CW01567075

JEFF STRAND

ADAM PEPPER

SARAH PINBOROUGH

JEFFREY THOMAS

DARKARt8

B O O K S

CONTENTS

INTRODUCTION

Good shit is where you find it.

The needle in the haystack, the diamond in the rough, the quarter in the mud puddle – wondrous treasures often await the lucky, the canny and the adventurous.

For those of you familiar with the works of Jeff Strand, Adam Pepper, Sarah Pinborough and Jeffrey Thomas, this book will surely be a welcome addition to your library – all four of these great authors collected under one cover!

But, for those of you who maybe only were acquainted with one or two of these individuals – or, best of all, are coming into this wholly fresh – you are the folks I truly envy.

Get ready for some good shit.

Back in the early 1990's, I was excited to go see a band I really dug at the venerable (and, alas, defunct) Lounge Ax here in Chicago. The opening act was some oddly-named outfit from Ohio called "Ass Ponys."

I figured I could safely arrive late.

Somehow, though, I got to the show early and was sitting there drinking a beer with my buddies and talking when the Ass Ponys took the stage. If memory serves, the first song was called "I Love Bob," and was about a girl who met a guy and in the heat of those heady early days of a love affair carved those eponymous words into her leg with a razor.

As you can imagine, that got my attention.

The Ponys played on, jangly pop rock set to stories of invented freaks, murderers and oddballs, with the occasional paens to such unlikely real-life individuals as Julia Pastrana and Ford Madox Ford ("The Fattest Poet Who Ever Lived!") – kind of like early R.E.M by way of Diane Arbus.

From that moment through the subsequent many years and six twisted genius albums later, I remain a diehard fan.

A similar thing happened when I saw my first Don Hertzfeldt short. I was there to see something else, when all of a sudden, I was blindsided by an unexpected bonanza of such proportions that I completely have forgotten what film I had gone to see in the first place.

What the hell do the Ass Ponys and Don Hertzfeldt have to do with a book of weird stories, you ask? To me, those are two examples of those rare happy epiphanies that occur when you encounter an artist that totally blows you away – when you least expect it.

As I said before, if you're familiar with Jeff's, Adam's, Sarah's or Jeffrey's work, then you at least have some sense of what lies ahead – truly original ideas flawlessly executed by four enormously talented writers.

However, if by some fortunate happenstance this book is your introduction to the gifted authors to follow, then you, my friend, are in for quite a treat.

You won't find any of the "usual" suspects here – no vampires, no werewolves, no smilingly hateful little children who kill their nannies. What you will find instead are some very disturbing tales that showcase the full range of what constitutes a "horror story."

Several of the stories involve body parts gone missing or astray. Some of these stories are funny, some are elegant, and some are just downright nasty. What I can promise you is that these tales do present a great snapshot of the remarkable scope these authors have.

This book, the one previous (*Candy in the Dumpster*) and the one forthcoming (*Sins of the Sirens*) are the literary version of the quaint sampler candy box – a chance for you to "taste" the work of various authors and see what is to your liking.

How do you know if these stories will be to your liking?

Stories often begin by the writer asking "what if…?" or "what would…?" The stories in this book are no different: you have, for example, Jeff Strand asking "What would be the best way to kill the most trick-or-treaters on Halloween?" Or Adam Pepper asking "What would one do to get back a kidney donated under false pretenses?" Or Sarah Pinborough asking "If a murder victim were cut into pieces, came back as a zombie and then smoked methamphetamine, would the smoke come out of all the places where they didn't quite fit together again?" Or Jeffrey Thomas asking "If one could be intimate with any person who had ever lived or died, who would one pick, and how would that turn out?"

You know, the very same questions you or I might ask.

Those questions continue, with three samples from each writer. We decided on the format of multiple stories from four authors as a chance to showcase several works from each writer's oeuvre. Hopefully, this sparks your interest to seek out the other published work available from these four writers – as well as whetting your appetite for other fiction as well.

At the end of the day, it's all about the "good shit" – in whatever form you find it. Coming up next are twelve stories that certainly qualify.

Here's to the good shit.

> *–Bill Breedlove*
> *February 2007*
> *Chicago*

GRAMMA'S CORPSE

P a looked mighty angry as he walked into Jamie's room, holding her report card. She'd been dreading this moment ever
since she flunked two spelling tests in a row. He'd grounded
her for three weeks the last time report cards went out, and on
that one her lowest grade had been a C.

"Do you mind explaining this to me?" he asked, waving the
paper at her.

Jamie lowered her eyes. "I did my best, Pa."

"Is that what you think? You think that getting a C in math
and a D in spelling is doing your best?"

"I got two A's."

"You got an A in PE. That don't count. I'm proud of you for
getting an A in science, but that's not what I'm talking about. I'm
talking about these C's and D's."

"I'm sorry."

"Sorry ain't gonna cut it."

"I'll try harder next time!"

"You just said you did your best. So you were lying. You did-
n't study hard enough and you were lazy. Ain't that right?"

Jamie slowly nodded her head. "Yes, Pa."

"Lazy kids need to be punished. Don't you agree?"

"Yes, Pa."

"Grounding you obviously don't work. Neither does taking
away your allowance. I guess the only punishment that'll teach
you a good enough lesson is if you sleep with Gramma's corpse
tonight."

"Pa, no!"

"Your ma and I discussed it already. You need to start taking
your schoolwork more seriously. So tonight you're going to bed
early, and Gramma's dead body is going to be there right next to
you."

"That's not fair!"

"Don't you try to tell me what's fair and what ain't. You're lucky it's only for one night. Do you want the same treatment we gave your brother?"

"No, sir." Matt had slept with Gramma's corpse for three nights after he got into a fight at school. One night for fighting, one night for disobeying the teacher when she told them to stop, and one night for losing.

"Good. You ain't watching no TV tonight. You sit here and you do your homework. If you finish it, do it again. We'll bring Gramma in at eight-thirty, so you'd better be ready."

Pa was always punctual, and it was exactly eight-thirty when he came back into her room, holding Gramma underneath the shoulders while Ma held her feet. Gramma was still wearing the red dress with white dots that she'd wore to her funeral, and her head lolled forward so that Jamie could only see her stringy gray hair.

"Pull down the covers," Pa told her. "Help us tuck Gramma in."

The awful smell was already filling her room. Pa had pumped something into Gramma's body "to keep the rotting down," but it made Jamie's nose burn, and Gramma's arms and legs looked a lot worse than they had when she died six weeks ago.

"Please, Pa, don't put her in my bed! I promise I'll get better grades next time! I'll study all night! I won't watch TV for the whole rest of the school year! Please!"

"Don't make me get out the belt, Jamie."

"I'll take the belt! You can belt me all you want! I'll go fetch it for you! That's a good punishment, right?"

"Dammit, I said to pull down the covers! Your Gramma's body ain't getting any lighter!"

Jamie wanted to cry, but that would make Pa even madder. Instead, she walked over to her bed and pulled down her pretty pink blankets with the horses on them. She'd never be able to sleep under them again.

"The sheets too!" said Pa.

Jamie pulled down the sheets. Ma and Pa gently lay Gramma's thin body down on the bed on her back, right in the middle. Pa moved Jamie's pillow to the center and rested Gramma's head on it. Her wrinkled, yellow face was pinched up in a scowl. (Jamie figured that *she'd* scowl, too, if her mouth was sewn shut.) Her eyes were closed.

"Go brush your teeth and get in your pajamas," said Ma, smiling kindly. "Wear the blue lacy ones that Gramma bought you for your birthday. She'll like that."

Pa gave Ma a dirty look. "Now, don't go acting like she's alive. This is a dead body that ain't got no preference on the pajamas. We've talked about this."

"I know, I know..."

Jamie got the blue pajamas out of her dresser drawer and went into the bathroom. She brushed her teeth for as long as she could, until Pa yelled at her to hurry up. Then she changed into her pajamas and slowly returned to her room.

Gramma was still scowling.

"Can't you move her over just a little?" Jamie asked.

Pa shook his head. "You two are sleeping *close*. That's the only way you'll learn your lesson. Now get in bed."

Jamie climbed into her small bed. The only way she could avoid touching Gramma was to have half of her body dangling off the side.

"Stop playing around!" said Pa. "You snuggle up tight to Gramma's corpse."

"I can't!"

"The hell you can't! Snuggle!"

"*Please*, Pa!"

"I'm gonna count to ten, and I'm gonna skip the first five. If you aren't all the way in bed you'll be sleeping with Gramma for the rest of the week!"

"Harold!" said Ma, shocked.

"I mean it! I won't tolerate no disrespect in my house! Six...seven..."

Jamie quickly scooted against Gramma's cold body. The smell made her want to throw up and she slapped her hand over her own nose and mouth.

"That's more like it. Now we'll be checking on you, and I expect to see both of you in that bed when we do. You lie there real still, and you think about what you've done, and you go to sleep. Understand?"

"Yes, Pa."

Ma pulled the covers up over both Jamie and Gramma. "Good night, sweetheart. We'll see you in the morning."

"Can I sleep with the light on?"

Pa shook his head. "No, but we'll leave the door cracked open so you get light from the hallway."

"Okay."

Ma and Pa both gave her a kiss on the forehead, and then they left the room. Pa closed the door almost all of the way, letting a single strip of light in across the bed, illuminating Gramma's wrists.

The smell was absolutely horrible. Jamie knew that she'd never get it out of her skin.

Gramma's flesh was chilly and moist. It was cold and wet down in the basement where Pa kept her, so that wasn't surprising. Jamie wondered how long it would take the dead body to at least warm up to room temperature.

She closed her eyes. If she could just fall asleep quickly, it would all be over, except for nightmares. She lay there, trying only to breathe through her mouth, and willed herself to fall asleep.

It wasn't working.

She'd never fall asleep next to a dead body. Even if Gramma smelled like candy and was warm like an electric blanket, she'd never be able to do it.

To be honest, Gramma had been scary before she died. She was always looking at invisible things and licking her lips. She also muttered under her breath, weird words that Jamie couldn't understand. Though she knew that it was bad, really bad, she was actually kind of relieved when Pa told her that God had taken Gramma away.

But just her soul. Not her body.

"No mother of mine is gonna be buried six feet under the dirt," Pa had said. "They did it to Grampa, but they aren't doing it to Gramma! They aren't gonna burn her up, either, and that's a promise!"

Ma and Pa had argued about it, but Pa told her that this was just the way things were going to be. He was going to respect her body until there was no body left to respect. He liked to fix up animals that he'd shot or caught in traps, even though some of them fell apart sometimes, and he'd been really proud when he showed Ma, Jamie, and Matt what he'd done with Gramma.

Most of the time they kept her in the basement. Sometimes they brought her upstairs to sit on the couch when the family watched TV. They never sat her down at the dinner table, though, because Pa said it was unhygienic.

Jamie squeezed her eyes shut as tightly as she could. She squeezed them shut until her eyelids ached, while she begged her mind to let her fall asleep.

Was somebody breathing?

She held her own breath and listened carefully.

She couldn't hear anything except the soft sounds of the TV from downstairs. She opened her eyes and stared at Gramma, watching carefully for a rise and fall of her chest in the shadows, but she wasn't moving.

Of course she wasn't. She was dead.

Gramma's corpse was still cold, and it was also kind of sticky. Jamie would've given almost anything just to be able to scoot away from her, but she had no doubt that Pa would make good on his threat to check on her, and there was no way she could handle sleeping with the body another night.

She lay there, staring at the ceiling. She tried to imagine horses galloping across the ceiling, splashing through a river, carrying her away from her bedroom into a beautiful meadow.

She thought she heard breathing again.

Jamie stared at Gramma, silently praying: *Don't open your eyes. Don't open your eyes. Please don't open your eyes.*

Gramma did not open her eyes. She didn't move at all.

Jamie wanted to cry, but she refused to. No matter what, she wasn't going to cry, and not just because it would make Pa angry. She was going to be brave. Gramma was dead. She couldn't hurt her, not even a little bit. This was *her* room, and *her* bed, and she wasn't going to let a dead old lady scare her anymore.

It was like the creepy doll Ma had got her last Christmas. At first it terrified her and made her cry, but Ma forced her to hold it, and after a while it wasn't so scary anymore. She'd just have to make Gramma's corpse less scary.

Her eyes were starting to adjust to the light, so she observed Gramma closely. Just a stupid ol' dead lady. It wasn't like she could come back to life and bite her. All she could do was lie there and stink. Matt stunk a lot of the time, and he wasn't the least bit scary.

Please don't open your eyes...

Jamie extended her index finger, and held it up to Gramma's nose. She hesitated for a several moments, gradually building up her courage, and then –

– no, she couldn't do it...

Yes, she could.

She poked Gramma on the nose. In her mind she made a "Boing!" sound.

Gramma didn't move.

See? Just a stupid dead body that couldn't hurt anybody. Jamie could do anything she wanted to it. She pinched Gramma's nose shut and started to count to ten.

She only made it to three before pulling her hand away in revulsion.

She'd never make it through the night. Never ever.

And now she had to go to the bathroom.

But she couldn't get up. If Pa heard her leave her room, he'd be furious, and if she did leave her room, Jamie didn't think she'd ever be able to crawl back into bed with that *creature*.

No, not that creature. Creatures could hurt you. This was just a dead body. A stupid, harmless, dumb-looking dead body.

She wondered if Gramma's spirit was in the room, watching over her body. Maybe her ghost was mad that Jamie had pinched the corpse's nose.

So what? A ghost couldn't do any more to her than a dead body could.

Gramma's corpse licked its lips.

No, it didn't. She'd imagined that. Gramma's mouth was sewn shut. It couldn't do anything. Nothing at all.

Why hadn't she studied harder?

Why hadn't she at least cheated on that spelling test?

She could feel herself starting to cry, but refused to let it happen. No way. Not a single tear.

Jamie lay quietly until the tremors in her chest subsided. She closed her eyes and tried to think about the horses again.

She felt something warm and slimy – a tongue – slide across her neck.

She gasped and opened her eyes, but Gramma's corpse lay still, exactly where it was before.

Thank God she hadn't screamed.

Jamie touched her neck in the spot where she'd felt the tongue. It was dry. Nobody had licked her. It was just her brain trying to scare her.

She hated Gramma.

She hated her rotten, smelly corpse. Probably full of bugs and worms. Maggots.

What if the bugs came out of Gramma while Jamie slept? What if they crawled into her ears and mouth?

Maybe she could pretend. She could scream for Pa, and say that a maggot came out of Gramma's nose. Pa wouldn't make her sleep with a corpse if maggots were coming out of it, would he?

No...but he'd know she was lying. He always did.

There were no bugs anyway. When Ma and Pa had argued about it, Pa said that the chemicals kept them away.

Stupid Gramma. Stupid dead Gramma. Jamie wanted to punch her in the face.

Why not?

If she was scared of her, why not punch her in the face? You couldn't be scared of something that you could beat up, could you?

Jamie clenched her right hand into a tight fist.

She shouldn't do it. Pa might find out. Or Gramma's ghost might get mad.

She didn't care.

She punched Gramma as hard as she could, right on the cheek. Her fist made a wet slapping sound as it hit, and one of Gramma's eyes popped open.

What had she done? Pa was going to kill her!

But Gramma didn't move. Not at all.

See? She couldn't hurt anybody. There was nothing to be scared of. She was like a big rag doll. And she wasn't so cold anymore.

Jamie was going to close her eyes, and she wasn't going to open them again until morning, no matter what. Maybe she'd ask to sleep with Gramma for a couple more hours, just to show Pa that he hadn't scared her.

She couldn't close her eyes. Not while Gramma's own eye was open. It was hard to see in the dark, but Gramma's eye didn't seem to have a pupil, it was just white.

Jamie very, very quickly put her finger on Gramma's eyelid and closed it, squealing as she accidentally touched the eyeball.

She froze, listening for Pa's footsteps.

Nothing.

She heard Matt laugh at something on TV.

Good. She was safe. Gramma's eye was closed again, and nothing could hurt her. Jamie closed her own eyes and lay still.

No sounds but her own breathing.

No tongue on her neck.

No teeth on her shoulder.

It was almost funny the way Pa thought he could teach her a lesson like this. Maybe she'd get *worse* grades on her next report card, just to show him what she thought of this punishment.

Jamie rolled over on her side. Gramma's arm came with her, wrapped around her waist.

Don't scream.

Without looking back, she lifted the dead arm and tossed it back on Gramma's chest.

Horses. Pretty horses, galloping away from here...

She imagined Gramma's laugh, a high-pitched, scratchy laugh that hurt Jamie's ears.

Was Gramma looking at her? Staring at the back of her neck?

Gramma was going to kill her. Gramma was going to lean over and take a big bloody bite out of her neck. "*Mmmmmmmmm,*" Gramma would say. "*So, so tasty!*"

No, she wouldn't.

Maybe she would.

Jamie realized that she was crying. She didn't remember when she'd started.

She didn't want to die.

She shouldn't have punched Gramma in the face.

Gramma's fingertips danced across Jamie's back. Gramma was licking her lips – Jamie knew it. Licking her lips and thinking about how delicious Jamie would taste.

No, no, no, no! She was not!

There were no fingers on Jamie's back.

Or on her neck.

It was a lie.

Please, please, please let me fall asleep...

When you fall asleep, I'm gonna get you...

NO!

Oh, yes, little Jamie. You never loved Gramma enough. You always turned your head when Gramma tried to give you a kiss? Why wouldn't you give your Gramma a kiss, Jamie? Why don't you make it up to her and give her a kiss right now?

Jamie slammed her hands over her ears.

Mmmmmmmm...Gramma's hungry...

Leave me alone!

Jamie didn't know if she'd screamed that out loud or in her mind.

She was sobbing now, and she didn't care if Pa heard her.

A hand grabbed her neck.

Squeezed.

This wasn't in her mind. She really couldn't breathe!

Jamie tried to call for help, Pa, Ma, Matt, anyone, but her voice wouldn't work. The fingers on her throat were too tight.

Gramma squeezed and squeezed.

Such a bad little girl...never studies, never does her homework...and doesn't love her Gramma...

"Please stop..." Jamie managed to say. She'd definitely said this out loud.

No, sweetie. I'll never stop until you're just like me. Just. Like. Me.

Jamie fell asleep.

✦ ✦ ✦

Jamie's hands were so tight around her own neck that Martin could barely pry them off. While his wife stood next to the bed, screaming, Martin checked his daughter for a heartbeat.

"My baby! My precious baby!" Patricia wailed. *"What have we done?"*

There was no heartbeat or pulse. His daughter was dead.

Patricia scooped up her tiny body and cradled it to her chest. *"My baby...my baby..."*

Martin just stood there, absolutely stunned.

Gramma lay on her back in the bed, unmoving.

Patricia looked at Gramma and continued to shriek. *"Why is she grinning like that? Dear God, why is she grinning?"*

BAD CANDY HOUSE

I don't get how the whole "razor blades in apples" thing is supposed to work. I think it's an urban legend. How could you get a razor blade in there without leaving a big gash in the side of the apple? I mean, yeah, kids are morons, but they're going to notice an inch-long cut in the side of their apple. I guess you could come in from the bottom, but using that technique I don't see how you could wedge the blade in far enough that somebody would actually bite into it. And there's really no set biting pattern for an apple, so unless you lucked into a direct hit the best you could hope for is a little nick on the lips – barely even worth the trouble. Most importantly, kids are going to remember the cheap bastards who handed out apples instead of candy (granted, an apple costs more than a Fun-Size candy bar, but that's not the way they see it) and they'll bring the police right to your front door.

It just wouldn't work.

That's why I used arsenic, injected with a hypodermic needle into name-brand chocolates. Even if parents checked the candy, they were unlikely to notice the holes, and the little cretins were sure to just pop those things into their greedy mouths whole. Dead kids. A Halloween present to myself.

I wasn't ignorant; I knew I wouldn't kill all of them. As soon as the first one croaked, there'd be mass hysteria all over town and parents would be yanking the bags of candy away from their screaming brats. But I figured I'd probably knock off a few of them before people started freaking out, and in a worst case scenario where I only killed one – well, hell, at least I'd be responsible for everybody else's candy being taken away. Heh heh.

Obviously, the candy would eventually be traced back to me. But that was fine. My Mildred had died two months ago, and I really didn't have anything to live for. I would've blown my brains out the same night the stroke took her, except that it occurred to me that if I didn't have to worry about any consequences to my actions, I could have one hell of an enjoyable Halloween.

I was downright giddy. I even carved a jack-o-lantern for the first time in thirty years. A jack-o-lantern was actually the source of my very first journal entry about the holiday:

October 31, 1975. Those little bastards smashed my jack-o-lantern. I hope they choke on their taffy.

I had something for pretty much every year after that.

October 31, 1985. Those little shits toilet-papered my entire front yard. I saw them running away and laughing, and I went for my shotgun, but Mildred talked some sense into me. I sort of wish she hadn't.

October 31, 1995. Those little fuckers put a burning bag of dog crap on my porch. I'm not an idiot and I wasn't going to just stomp on the thing, so I turned the water hose on it and put out the fire. It left burn marks on the wood that those little fuckers are going to pay for, believe me. Then when I picked it up to throw it away, the wet bag broke and spilled shit all over. I went for my shotgun, but Mildred had hidden the bullets. I saw the kids watching from across the street, and I gave them a verbal beating that they won't soon forget. I hate kids.

October 31, 2005. Those little satanists egged the whole goddamn front of my house. Where the hell did they get all those eggs? One of them threw a fuckin' ham and cheese omelet at my window. Can you believe that? A ham and cheese omelet! I swear to God, if Mildred hadn't pawned my shotgun, I'd just sit down on my porch and start picking those little demons off one by one. Boom! Splat! Boom! Splat! Boom! Splat! I hate Halloween.

But I didn't hate Halloween this year. I couldn't wait to see what they tried. Eggs, toilet paper, burning bags of crap...bring it on! This might be the last Halloween our sleepy little shithole town ever enjoyed.

At 6:44, the doorbell rang. Trick-or-treating was supposed to officially start at 7:00, but those greedy bastards didn't care.

I opened the door. Two kids were standing there, holding their candy bags out in front of them expectantly. One was in vampire makeup and the other wore a Spider-Man mask.

I stared at them. They just stood there, too lazy to even say "trick or treat!" Why don't kids say "trick or treat" anymore? Was the process of securing Halloween candy so difficult that they had to figure out a way to cut down on the manual labor? These rotten kids today have such a feeling of entitlement that they can't even be bothered to say those three words to get their damn candy bar.

They didn't even say "Hi." They just looked at me, slack-jawed, as if they didn't have two brain cells to rub together. (To be fair, I couldn't see the kid's face under his Spider-Man mask, but I don't think it's unreasonable to assume that he looked as stupid as his vampire buddy.)

"Yeah?" I asked.

"Trick or treat," said the bloodsucker, as if annoyed that I was making him fulfill his part of the bargain.

I picked two chocolates from the bowl next to the door and dropped one into each of their bags. "Enjoy," I said, wanting to add "your upcoming death" but wisely withstanding the temptation.

The vampire muttered "thank you" under his breath and they left. I smiled, which was not something I did often. I wondered if they'd realize that the chocolate tasted funny, or if they'd gobble it down too fast to even notice.

"Oooooh, Mommy, I don't feel so good."

"You've just had too much Halloween candy, sweetie-dumplings. Let me tuck you under the covers and give you a kiss and you'll be just fine in the morning."

"But my tummy hurts."

"Maybe you've learned a little lesson for next year. You shouldn't eat so much candy. It's not good for you."

"Bleaaarrrrrgggghhhh."

"Oh my God! You're vomiting blood! You're vomiting blood! Mike, come quick!"

"[Various frothing at the mouth noises.]"

"Good Lord, Tracy, what did he eat? What did you let him eat?"

"It wasn't my fault, you son of a bitch! If you'd helped teach our children some respect, this wouldn't be happening! I hate you I hate you I hate you I hate – AAAAIIIEEEEE, his tongue just fell out! His tongue just fell right out of his mouth!"

"Gagghhhrrrruuuuummmppphhhhh..."

"Speak to me! Speak to me, little vampire! He's dead! He died a horrible and agonizing death! Noooooooooo!!!"

"Nooooooooooo!!!"

Hee hee hee.

Nine minutes later, the doorbell rang again. Two teenage girls were there. They looked way too old to be trick-or-treating, and were probably just collecting candy to sell for drug money. Not only did they not say "trick or treat," but the spoiled debutantes weren't even wearing costumes.

I shook my head. "You can't have candy without a costume." Yes, it was poisoned candy, so their lack of proper attire shouldn't have been a concern for me, but this was just ridiculous.

"We *are* in costume," said the blonde on the left.

"What are you supposed to be? Teenage girls scamming candy?"

"I'm Paris Hilton," said the blonde on the right. "She's Jessica Simpson."

"Paris Hilton? Shouldn't you be having sex in Night-Vision?" The computer and Internet connection had been Mildred's thing, not mine, but after she died I'd discovered the convenience of internet porn.

"You are such a pervo," said the one who was supposed to be Jessica Simpson.

"I'm not the one dressing up in slut gear," I said.

"Well, thank God for that," said Paris.

"I'm going to tell my parents about you," Jessica threatened. "They lock away creeps like you."

"All right, all right, here's your candy," I said, giving them two pieces each. "Great costumes. You look just like them. Now go away."

The girls exchanged a disgusted look and then left. I chuckled. I probably shouldn't have harassed them – if their parents did come over and cause problems I might not get to distribute enough of the chocolates – but it was fun.

The flood of kids started a few minutes after that. I smiled politely, complimented their costumes, and enjoyed merry thoughts about their deaths. I fantasized about horrified parents having to walk around the bodies littering the streets, unable to cross the street without accidentally stepping on a youthful corpse. I knew it wouldn't happen like that, but it was enjoyable to pretend.

A mother showed up, holding a baby in her arms. The baby had kitten whiskers drawn on its face and wore a pair of fake feline ears. It was too young to even hold the plastic pumpkin by itself – the mother held it instead. Did she think a baby could appreciate the holiday? I dropped a poisoned chocolate into the pumpkin. A mother stupid enough to give chocolate to a baby deserved whatever happened.

I'd given out about half of the bowl when three kids showed up at my door. They were all tall enough to be teenagers, although their identical skeleton masks hid their faces.

"Gimme candy, old man!" they said in unison.

"Oh, that's real clever. You make that up yourselves?"

"You gonna give us the candy or what?"

"Yeah, I'm gonna give you the candy," I said, dropping one in each of their bags. "Happy Halloween."

Suddenly, all three of them pulled out squirt guns. Before I could react, they squirted me in the face.

I slammed the door and cursed loudly. I cursed even louder as the smell made it abundantly clear that the squirt guns weren't filled with water.

"Damnfuckin'bastardhellspawnmonsters!" I shouted as I rushed to the kitchen sink and turned on the faucet. If I weren't planning to kill myself tonight, I would've gone to the police station first thing in the morning and demanded DNA testing on the urine.

This was exactly why they all needed to die. You couldn't shoot a man in the face with bodily fluids and expect to live through the night.

Rotten bastards. Rotten twerps. Rotten brats. I hated them all. I wished that I could just walk through their homes, spraying piss-scented arsenic into their wide-open mouths.

Maybe I wouldn't kill myself tonight. I'd stay alive long enough to enjoy their fatal reaction to my treats. Hell, maybe I'd go on the run for a few days, but return to laugh and point during their funerals. Walk up to their dead bodies in the open casket and squirt them in the face.

Good times.

I ignored the next couple of doorbell rings while I thoroughly washed my face with soap. My left eye stung a bit, and a drop or two seemed to have gone up one of my nostrils, but at least none had made it into my mouth.

Nice and clean, I returned to my door-answering duties. The next kid actually said the magic words and politely thanked me for his chocolate, so I hoped that he'd hear about the other deaths before he ate the piece I'd given him. I gave out chocolate to Elvira, Freddy Krueger, another vampire, a toddler clown, a Mexican wrestler, some *Star Wars* character (I think), and two separate kids dressed as M&Ms, which I wouldn't have expected to be a popular costume choice.

I was almost out of candy and ready to shut down for the night when somebody rang the doorbell over and over, getting in about fifteen rings before I could answer. Officially, trick-or-treating was supposed to end at nine o'clock, and it was nine o'three, so I felt that I'd be justified in punching this little shit in the face.

I opened the door and saw a kid in a skeleton mask. The same mask those other three kids had been wearing. I wasn't sure if he'd been part of that group, but I hated him anyway.

"Trick or treat!" he said in a monotone.

"Yeah, yeah, whatever," I muttered, watching his hands carefully to make sure he didn't whip out a squirt gun. I dropped one of the last pieces of candy into his bag. "Happy Halloween."

The kid nodded but didn't move.

"Something you want?" I asked.

The kid just stood there, staring silently at me. I don't mind admitting that it was more than a little creepy.

"You've got your candy," I told him. "Go on, get back home, it's late."

More silence. More staring.

I put my hand on the edge of the door so I could slam it in his face. "Do you know who I am?" he asked.

"No. Who are you?"

"I am the one under the mask. I am the one who sees all. I know your secrets, Raymond."

"Get the hell off my porch."

"You cannot escape what you have done."

"I haven't done shit."

"Do you wish to gaze under my mask, or do you fear the visage that hides beneath?"

"Go away, you little freak."

He shook his head, slowly and deliberately. "You must confront what you have done, Raymond. Remove my mask. Look upon that which rests behind the disguise."

What the hell is going on here? Something about this kid (it *was* a kid, right?) made me extremely uncomfortable. I didn't want to touch his mask, I just wanted him to leave, and yet I felt myself reaching out and touching the cool plastic.

I started to lift the mask.

And then a warm stream of piss got me right on the fucking lips. I stumbled backwards, sputtering in surprise and fury, as the son of a bitch squirted me again.

"Sucker!" he shouted.

I'm an old man, but unspeakable rage does a lot for one's ability to move fast. I rushed forward, ignoring the third squirt that got in my hair, and grabbed the kid by the collar. I dragged him inside, threw him to the living room floor, and slammed the front door.

"It was just a joke!" the kid insisted.

"A joke, huh?" I asked, wiping my mouth off on my sleeve. "Then shouldn't at least one of us be laughing? Isn't that part of what makes a joke a joke?"

"I – I don't know!"

"What if I made you squirt yourself in the mouth? Would that be funny? Would you be slapping your knee over that little joke?"

"No!"

"Are you sure? I think it would be hilarious! I'd bust a fuckin' gut! Give me the squirt gun."

The kid quickly tossed me the squirt gun. I pointed it at him and pulled the trigger, but it was almost empty and only a few drops trickled out, landing on my shoes and carpet. This did not improve my mood.

"I bet you helped egg my house last year, didn't you?" I asked.

The kid shook his head.

"Take off the mask!"

He quickly pulled off the skeleton mask and threw it aside. He was one terrified looking kid. I approved of that. He looked about sixteen and was making a valiant but ineffective attempt to grow a mustache.

"Did you egg my house last year?"

"No!"

"Liar!"

"I didn't!"

The kid started to get back up, but I pounced upon him. I was pleased with my own strength as I grabbed him by the ears and slammed his head against the floor, over and over, until he stopped moving.

I checked his pulse. Not dead.

Good.

I hurried into the kitchen, opened the drawer where I kept random junk, and got a roll of duct tape. Quickly, before he could regain consciousness, I taped his wrists together and his feet together. The doorbell rang during this process, but I ignored it.

I woke him up with a slap to the face.

"What's your name?" I asked.

"Gary."

"Gary, why did you make the decision to squirt me in the face with urine? Did you think that was a nice thing to do?"

"It wasn't my idea!"

"Was it your urine?"

"No."

"Okay. I'm sure you wouldn't lie about such a thing. I'll be right back."

I returned to the kitchen and got a carton of eggs out of the refrigerator. Then I walked back into the living room, set the carton on the coffee table, opened the lid, and held up one of the eggs to show Gary.

"For true revenge, this thing should be rotten. But I don't want to keep you in my house long enough for these to go bad."

I threw the egg at him, as hard as I could. It splattered on his chest. I'd been aiming for his face, but that was okay. I pelted the rest of the eggs, feeling a rush of adrenaline with each throw. He lay there, covered with yolk and egg shells, and it was one of the most beautiful sights I'd ever witnessed.

Next, I grabbed some spare rolls of toilet paper out of the closet. I wrapped him up like a mummy, kicking him a few times when he struggled too much. I held the last roll under running water for a minute, then smushed it against his face.

I didn't have any dog crap handy. In theory, there was no rule saying that a dog had to be involved, and I briefly considered another option, but then I decided that I had too much dignity. Besides, I figured that the kid himself was nothing more than a piece of crap, so why not treat him that way?

Oh, he screamed good when I lit him on fire.

Even though it was Halloween and people were used to kids screaming, I knew he'd attract unwanted attention before too long. As he flailed around on the ground, burning and shrieking, I noticed that his head bore a striking resemblance to one of my old jack-o-lanterns that kids had smashed.

A few blows with a baseball bat and he resembled it even more.

I sat down on the couch to relax, and got so caught up in staring at his body that the arrival of the police took me by surprise. They carted me away and put me under twenty-four hour surveillance, so my whole plan to kill myself was botched.

Sadly, I hadn't planned for police intervention this soon, and so I hadn't really covered my tracks. They discovered the syringe and arsenic, and quickly went door-to-door telling people not to eat any Halloween candy. The only casualty was the baby in the kitten costume.

I have to admit, knowing that I'll spend the rest of my life in prison is nowhere near as appealing as suicide. I keep trying to get rope or a knife or something, but the guards are watching me good. I guess I won't be seeing Mildred anytime soon.

The worst part is that, as a prank, the guards keep toilet-papering my cell. They've also hung up Halloween decorations, and the worst of them, Steve, just loves to knock on the bars and say "Trick or treat, asshole!"

That said, I'd do it all over again if I could. It was still the best Halloween of my life.

"HERE'S WHAT HAPPENED..."

S o I'm sitting in Harvey's Diner, okay? It's me and Joey, and it's about eleven-thirty at night, and there are...I dunno, maybe ten other people in the restaurant. The waitress is hot but she's pretty much incompetent, and we've been waiting for almost fifteen minutes just to get a cup of coffee.

You know Joey, he's all like "Let's just go!" but that's stupid. Even if it takes her another fifteen minutes to bring us our coffee, that's still less time than it would take to find another place that's open this late. And you know Harvey's – their food is borderline poison, but they make great coffee. None of that $3.95-for-a-small-cup-with-fifteen-words-in-the-name nonsense. It's hot, black, and they'll refill it all night without complaining. Good stuff.

Anyway, we're sitting there waiting, and I forget what else we were talking about. Movies, I think. Some romantic comedy his girlfriend made him see. No, it wasn't that one. He didn't see it in the theatre – I think it just came out on DVD. No, it had that one chick from that sitcom, the one where they're at work. The redhead. She was in that other movie that won the Academy Award. No, it wasn't that. Ah, it doesn't matter.

We're sitting there talking, and then the chef pushes through the swinging door from the kitchen. He's wearing this apron that's got streaks of red on it, and he's holding – I swear – a meat cleaver. Not a bloody meat cleaver, but it's a frickin' meat cleaver, and he's holding it up like he's ready to whack it into somebody's head! And he walks down the aisle, stomping his feet, and he goes "Who sent back the goddamn turkey sandwich?"

No, it definitely wasn't Julia Roberts in the movie. She was never in a sitcom. I'm trying to tell you about the chef with the meat cleaver, okay? Yeah, I know she was in one episode of *Friends*, but that's not what I'm talking about. No, it wasn't Sandra Bullock. You're missing the point of my story.

So the chef is holding this meat cleaver and he wants to know who sent back the turkey sandwich. And Joey is all tensed up and looking like he wants to bolt, but at this point I figure we're okay, since neither one of us ordered a turkey sandwich. And the chef starts walking past the tables. He's this bald guy with a really big gut, but he looks *strong*, y'know? Like, you have to assume that if he did bring that cleaver down on your skull, it would crack through a couple of inches of bone, easy.

And we see this one guy looking really nervous, and there's no question at all that he's the poor schmuck who sent back the sandwich. Have you ever had a sandwich there? I've never had the turkey, but the roast beef was rubbery and the tomatoes were all slimy and the bread was stale. So I don't blame the guy one bit for sending his back. He just picked a really bad night to do it.

Jesus, I'm sorry I brought up the romantic comedy! It's not important! Just forget I said anything about it and try to focus on – yes, that was it! No, I didn't see it, but Joey said it sucked.

The chef walks right up to the guy's table. This lady is sitting across from him – maybe his wife, I'm not sure – and she's staring at the chef with bugged-out eyes and her jaw hanging open and a milk mustache. And here's the part that's gonna mess with your mind. The chef screams "How do you like this turkey sandwich?" and then – *thwack!* – he slams the meat cleaver right into the guy's face!

I'm not lying, I swear! He whacked it into his nose! Joey and I, we're all like "Holy cow, the chef's gone berserk!" and the guy's wife or girlfriend or whatever is screaming and crying and people start jumping up from their tables and freaking out. The guy with the cleaver in his face, he's not dead. He's hollering "My nose! My nose!" but it sounds all funny because he's got a cleaver in his nose, y'know? You can't really blame the guy for being upset.

Then the chef yanks the meat cleaver out, and...you wanna hear something gross? This is really nasty. The guy must've had a bad cold. There's this big string of snot on the blade along with all the blood, and it stretches out like cheese on a pizza. Oh, man, I thought I was gonna puke!

So now I'm thinking, what do I do? Should I call the cops? Should I run? Should I try to save the poor bastard?

What? I don't know why he didn't put his hand up to block the cleaver. Yeah, I guess it should've been instinctive, but he didn't do it. I didn't get a chance to ask him! It wasn't the kind of situation where I'm going to stroll over there and say "Excuse me, kind sir, but if I might borrow a moment of your time, I'd like to know why you didn't elect to use your hand to deflect the meat cleaver." I don't care if it doesn't make any sense – I'm just telling you what I saw, okay? He was dead in the next few seconds anyway.

Damn it, now you're making me get ahead of the story.

So the chef swings his arm back, and then *whack*! Slashes the cleaver right across the guy's throat! Joey and I are both like, no way did that just happen! And then I start to think that maybe the whole thing is a publicity stunt, y'know? Like maybe Harvey's is trying to cater to edgier clientele, so they're faking homicides. But then I realize that there's just no way. The guy is spraying blood everywhere, his wife or girlfriend is shrieking, and most of the other people in the restaurant are running for the exit.

Joey looks me right in the eye and he says, totally calmly, "Dude, this is really messed up."

What do you mean, how could I hear him over the other noise? Are you *trying* to be a jerk? I've got this great story, and you just want to sit there and poke holes in it. Well, screw you. I've got better things to do than talk to you if you're going to act this way.

Oh, that's *real* mature. What a class act you are. I don't care if you ever hear the end of the story or not, so that doesn't bother me a bit.

Okay, look, could you at least let me tell the next part without interrupting me? You're not gonna believe what happened.

People have made it to the door, and they're trying to push it open, and this lady screams "It's locked! It's locked! Oh my God, they've locked us in!"

Can you believe that? A chef storming out of the kitchen and attacking a restaurant patron I can maybe understand, but they locked us in! How demented is that?

The turkey sandwich guy is all flopped back in his seat, gurgling and clutching at his throat. The chef grabs the guy's wife/girlfriend by the hair, bashes her down on the table, and slams the meat cleaver into the back of her neck. I don't think she even ordered a turkey sandwich! Now the chef is a big guy, but he couldn't get all the way through her head in one blow, so he does it again and again and again.

Finally I turn away, because there are only so many times you can watch somebody try to chop somebody's head off, y'know? And people are trying to grab chairs and tables to break through the windows, but the chairs and tables are all bolted to the floor at Harvey's, so people are just shouting "Oh no! The tables and chairs are all bolted to the floor!" I think at this point Joey and I are the only ones left in our seats, if you don't count the guy and girl that the chef already killed.

People start kicking and slamming their fists against the glass, but it's not glass! It's plastic. Or maybe that's not actually plastic...it's just the clear stuff you use that doesn't break. I'm not a restaurateur so I'm not sure. But these people have now gone completely out of their minds. It's *nuts*, man.

I look back at the chef, and he finally got the woman's head off. And my stomach gets all twisted up because I think he's gonna do something completely disgusting and flat-out wrong with the head, but he just knocks it off the table. It bounces a little.

At this point, I'm disturbed but I'm not too concerned about my own personal safety. I mean, yeah, the chef has a meat cleaver, but it's not like he can chop off all of our heads, right? If the crowd would've rushed him instead of getting all bent out of shape over the locked door, we probably could've saved the headless woman.

Then the other chef walks out.

He's got a frickin' *rifle!*

Now even I'm starting to question the motivations that are going on here at this point. I start to think that it may not be about that turkey sandwich.

Bang! A guy who was pounding on the window gets the back

of his head blown open. No multiple whacks with a meat cleaver for this guy – he's dead.

Bang! Another guy dead!

Bang! This old lady gets it in the back!

Now, if this were a made-up story, I'd talk about how brave I was and stuff, but I'm not making any of this up. So Joey and I, we got our butts right under that table, and we did it quick! And I can hear the rifle going off: Bang! Bang! Bang!

No, I'm not sure what kind of rifle it was. I don't know guns very well. It was brown and it had a leather strap, I think.

Joey and I hear footsteps, and we can tell that the other chef is running across the diner. Bang! Bang! We're not hearing as much screaming anymore, if you know what I mean. Bang! Bang!

Joey goes "We have to do something!"

I go "What?"

Joey goes "Anything!"

I go "But what?"

Joey goes "I don't know! Something!"

I go "I agree, but what?"

There's maybe another six or seven shots, and then that's it. No more noise. They've slaughtered everybody else in the place. Joey and I are huddled under the table, trying to be very, very quiet, although since Harvey's is a pretty small place and there aren't tablecloths hanging down to cover us or anything it's a safe bet that we're gonna be found.

And this really sucked: Joey's cell phone went off.

It's sort of a double-whammy, y'know? Not only did the phone give away our position, tenuous as it might have been, but it made us realize that we'd been too stupid to use our cell phones to call the cops when we had a chance. We're all like, *d'oh!*

So I hear footsteps running, and suddenly there's the chef, pointing the rifle under the table. And he –

Oh. I think the restroom's in the back, right next to the dartboard. Sure, no problem.

Hmmmm-hmmm-hmmm. La-de-da.

Yeah, I'll have another one. Thanks.

Hmmmm-hmmm-hmmm.

Jesus, how long does it take? You're not building a frickin' ark in there.

Hey, welcome back! Where did I leave off?

No, no, I was way past the meat cleaver decapitation. Then what's the last part you remember? I know I told you about the rifle. The second chef came out and he started shooting everybody. Me and Joey hid under the table. Then Joey's cell phone went off and the chef was right there with the rifle. I don't know what kind. I told you, it was brown with a strap.

I have no idea who was calling Joey. He didn't answer because he was a bit too preoccupied with the rifle-toting chef. So the chef says "Get the hell out from under there." And neither Joey nor I particularly *want* to do it, but we also don't want to join the other people who've got bullets in them, know what I mean? We're both kind of hesitant, because I figure that whoever comes out first is gonna get shot first, and I'm guessing that Joey figures the same thing, and we aren't quite prodding each other, but we're definitely trying to use non-verbal communication to suggest that the other person should go first.

And the chef is like "*Now!*" and so Joey scoots out from under the table. But the chef doesn't shoot him, which immediately makes me wish I'd come out first. He just pushes him out of the way and then looks at me. I climb out from under there and stand up.

The whole place looks like there was a massacre. 'Cause there was one. I mean, there's blood all over the floor, blood dripping off the tables, blood splattered all over the windows, corpses all askew...it's sick.

The bald chef with the meat cleaver walks over and stands next to his friend. And they're just staring at us sort of funny, like maybe they're thinking "Shoot or cleave? Shoot or cleave?"

Joey goes "Why are you doing this?" Which is a pretty legitimate question, you've got to admit, but it also sounds kind of hokey. But I don't tell him that because I want to know the answer.

The rifle chef says "We're sick of people complaining about our food." And then he goes off on this rant that I swear lasted a good ten minutes. I mean, if you make crappy food and charge people for it, they're gonna call you on it sometimes, right? But,

God, he just went on and on and on, babbling about the lack of respect his customers give him, and how he worked his way through culinary school while he was taking care of his dying sister, and how nobody knew what kind of pressure he was under, and blah, blah, blah. By the end of his speech I was ready for a meat cleaver to the face.

Then he points his rifle back and forth between me and Joey, like he's trying to decide which one of us to shoot. And I'm trying to do this thing where I subtly move my eyeballs in Joey's direction, so that it might be some sort of subconscious signal that he should be the one to get shot. I mean, I don't wish Joey any harm or anything, but if one of us has to get shot, why not make it him, right?

The chef shoots Joey.

Not in the face or stomach – right in the kneecap. I cringe like he shot me instead, because I can't even imagine how much that's gotta hurt, although Joey's wailing is a pretty good clue. And the cleaver chef pushes Joey into the booth, laughing like he's gone completely insane. And Joey is bawling and shouting "Why me?" and now *both* chefs are laughing and the situation is so messed up that I can hardly even describe it.

The one chef twirls his cleaver and *whack!* There goes Joey's pinky. And the other chef presses the barrel of the rifle against the detached pinky and shoots it right off the table! Then they both laugh some more.

Is this too gross for you? It gets worse.

Pretty soon there's a pile of nine fingers on the table. The chef pushes them together into a nice tight pile, and then the other chef shoots again, sending fingers flying everywhere. And my first instinct is to bend down and try to scoop them up, just in case Joey lives through this and surgeons can re-attach them, but I don't want to call attention to myself.

Then the chef starts slicing up his arms. No, Joey's arms, not his own. Duh. The cleaver isn't going through the bigger bones too well – it's probably dull from all the work he's put it through. I can't help but wonder if he'd offer me some kind of immunity if I went and got the blade sharpener for him, but of course I'm not really gonna ask that.

Then I guess they got tired of Joey making so much noise, because the other chef shoves the barrel of his revolver into Joey's mouth and pulls the trigger. And as all this stuff comes out, I swear to God my first thought was that I should gather it up in case the surgeons can sew it back in. Your mind does funny things under stress.

So Joey's dead. And since I'm the only non-sociopath left alive in the place, I figure I'm next. And, yep, my fears are confirmed when that rifle is suddenly pointed in my direction.

No, they didn't kill me. Are you trying to be a smart-ass? I'm telling you a story where one of my best friends got chopped up right before my eyes, and you're making fun of it. Oh, you thought I might be a ghost, real funny. Hilarious.

I'm almost done with the story. Can you find it within yourself to let me finish? I promise I won't take up much more of your ever-so-extremely-valuable time.

So I see my chance. The chefs are still laughing like maniacs, and I realize that the one with the rifle is only about eighty percent focused on me. That's when I kick him as hard as I can, right square in the upper thigh. And we struggle for a few minutes, and meanwhile the other chef slams his cleaver right into my arm. You can see the scar there, see? It's kind of faint. I'm not sure why it's jagged – that's just the way the meat cleaver hit it.

I get the rifle away from him, and *kaboom*! Right in the forehead! That chef is *history*, man! But there's no time for me to celebrate my victory, because the other chef is coming at me with that damn cleaver again.

I shout "This one's for Joey, you son of a bitch! And everybody else!" and pull the trigger.

Click. Rifle's empty.

So I bash the shit out of him with it. A lot messier, but it gets the job done.

And then the incompetent waitress from before comes out of the back room, looking all scared and stuff. She runs over and throws her arms around me and says "Thank you! Thank you so much! I was sure they were going to kill me next! Oh, I just don't know how I can repay you for what you've done!"

I tell her.

She looks at me, and starts to unbutton her blouse. I toss the rifle onto the floor, pull the waitress close to me, and –

Where the hell are you going?

This is the best frickin' part!

Ah, screw it. That's what happened.

THE ADMIRER

I like the way she walks from the bar to her car, east to west swagger in her hips; I can't help but stare – all the guys do. I love the way she smells, when I have the nerve to get close. Sometimes I listen to her, talking to her friend with a cute snorty giggle. I love to hear her voice. She comes here every Friday, and every Friday I follow her to her car: A two door sporty thing with a ribbon and tassels hanging from the mirror.

There's plenty of pretty girls here, but there's something in particular about *her*. There's something in particular, I don't know what it is. She doesn't know my name just yet. But I know in my heart: I've *got* to make her mine!

Most nights she leaves alone, but tonight she's leaving with *him*. He's everything I'm not: Strong and handsome. His hair has gel, his ears have diamonds and his arms have trendy, tribal tattoos.

I follow them to her place. She just met this guy, and yet his hands are *all* over her.

"Stop it!" I hear her say, but that cutesy giggle tells me she doesn't mean it.

He knows too, because he grabs her and carries her to the door. Suspended in his arms, she puts her key in the lock, and the two disappear inside.

Soon after, a light upstairs comes on, and I see her flawless silhouette.

"Come on up and climb me," Big Oak Tree, that runs along the side of her house says, in a tone so affable, I have to smile back and say, "Thank you, Big Oak Tree. I will."

"You can see everything from atop my branches," Big Oak Tree says.

Big Oak Tree is right. Once up in his hearty branches, I can see into her room with ease. They don't bother to dim the lights or close the blinds. They're too busy tearing off clothes while drooling on each other.

He removes her tube top, and I see how incredible her breasts are – even better than I imagined. As is her bottom half. Her legs are slender, but not too slender. Her hips are full and round, but not too full, nor too round. She is stunning…absolute perfection.

I cannot hear her through the closed window, but she yells something like, "Come get me, big daddy!"

"Fuck yeah!" he yells back, or something equally inarticulate. He is not perfection; he is far from it.

They don't use the bed, instead sinking towards the floor. His ass pops in and out of view, but I can't see her any longer.

"Thank you, Big Oak Tree," I say as I shimmy down.

"You're welcome. Come back soon."

"I will."

I walk down the alley beside her house and pass dented garbage cans.

"Hey! Look in here!" Tin Trashcan calls to me.

"Thank you, Tin Trashcan. I will."

Inside, I find used tampons and condoms. "Yuck!" I cry, about to walk away.

"No. Keep looking," Tin Trashcan insists.

So I keep searching for a morsel – any item from her life will do. I find a copy of her phone bill. "Karen," I say her first name aloud. "Karen," I repeat.

✶   ✶   ✶

"Hello," she says when I call her the following day. "Hello?"

I don't know what to say. She hangs up, but I call back.

"Hello!"

Oh that bubbly voice, even when she's nervous. I've got to make her mine!

I love her. I need her. She'll love me. She'll need me. I love her. I need her! I know that I'm good for her!

There's something in particular about her, to you it may seem strange, but I'm back up Big Oak Tree, staring at her window, and today, Nice Window is open.

"Come closer," Nice Window says.

"Yeah, go closer," Big Oak Tree agrees.

"Yeah, she wants it!" Tin Trashcan adds.

"Yes, I want you," Karen says, wearing just bra and panties. "Come on up here big fella."

"Me?" I say. Could she really mean it?

"Yes, you," she laughs, but *with* me, not *at* me, like all the others do.

I climb higher. The branches are thinner, but still support me. I am at Nice Window, looking in at her, yet I hesitate.

"Go on," Big Oak Tree encourages.

"Yeah! She wants it." Tin Trashcan barks.

I've got to make her mine!

"Well?" she asks with a shrug, pressing her boobs together perfectly, "are you coming?"

"Sure!" I say, climbing through Nice Window.

She screams!

BURIED A MAN I
HATED THERE

The drive is always the best part. The anticipation. The tingles in my fingertips. The sweat in my palms. I wipe my hands on my pants while peeking in the rearview to see my clean-shaven reflection; a picture of them hangs from the mirror, bouncing off the dash. The weather is nice – balmy; the February snow is melting a bit.

It may seem strange that I should find joy in this ride, being what it is and all…but I do. I always do. Stranger still, perhaps, is that the four-hour drive is the only time I'm happy. Ever. I suffer through three hundred and sixty-four miserable days and twenty hours a year simply for these four hours. When I'm in my car on the way there, I am happy. This is the tenth year I'm making this trip, and I plan to make many more. I will make this trip every year on this day until the day I die. That is a promise I made to them ten years ago. That is a promise I will never break.

She will be waiting there for me, I am quite sure. She is very dependable. She was always the reliable sister. The good sister. My wife, Jessica was the wild one. Not too wild, thank you very much. But when we first met she could be really impulsive. I remember once watching the midnight showing of…ah, hell, I don't even remember what movie it was. But I do remember sitting in the back row staring at the screen, but not really staring – more like looking in that general direction. Jessica's hand slid under my shirt, then down into my pants. Well, you can guess the rest but suffice it to say it was a good thing the theatre wasn't very crowded.

Heidi, on the other hand, was always, and still is the reliable twin. My wife's identical twin and every bit the spitting image. I mean identical. I could tell them apart, of course, but not by look-ing at them. They look that much alike. Light brown hair, hazel eyes, shapely curves like a woman should have – thin but not too thin. Funny though, when you get to know people – even twin sisters who grew up together and shared a bedroom for nineteen years – there are always little quirks and gestures that make them unique. Jessica talked more, and smiled more, too. Heidi has a certain glare when she gets mad or annoyed that only she can do. Jessica's voice was a hair higher in pitch. There are always little things that make up the individual. Those quirks should never be taken for granted; they should be cherished.

I pull up Route 9 East in Brattleboro the same way I always do. The same way I've done for the last ten years. The same way I did that day, when I frantically searched for them…then found them.

Right off Route 9 is a side road. It's a great shortcut that saves about ten miles off the drive if you're heading northeast. I make a right turn onto it. Cherry Hill Road, it's called. It's a dirt road – doesn't see much traffic. I pull to the side and park my car right next to the telephone pole. There are only two houses on Cherry Hill Road, and only one telephone pole.

I get out of my Honda and start up the path. I used to drive one of those SUVs with a nice burgundy paint job. Now I drive a plain black Honda. The SUV was great when I had a kid. Roomy, so all her toys wouldn't clutter things up. Plenty of storage in the back, 'cause even a weekend trip with a kid means lots of baggage. And best of all, the DVD player. Man! When you make the four-hour drive from just north of the city to Brattleboro, Vermont, that DVD player is golden. Used to keep Emily busy the entire ride. And busy meant quiet. Sure, I got sick of watching the same Elmo video over and over again – it was only half an hour long. But it was worth it.

There's a big field just off Cherry Hill Road with a *Private Property* sign out front, but no one ever bothers us. Every year, Heidi and I meet in the field and have a picnic. It isn't a celebra-tion, but she tries to treat it like one.

"Hi, Jack," Heidi says with a wide smile – a genuine one. She isn't capable of being anything but genuine. Heidi is happy to see me. It's a nice sentiment, but it isn't one we share.

"Hi," I say back. I smile too, but mine isn't sincere.

She knows. She looks down at the ground. For a few moments there's a painfully awkward silence as we stare at a puddle of melted snow. Then she says, "You got your nice shoes all wet and muddy."

"I know." I take a handkerchief out of the breast pocket of my suit and wipe my shoes off.

"I made all of your favorites."

"Great!" I shout with way too much enthusiasm.

She reaches into her wicker picnic basket and takes out a red and white checkered tablecloth. She tosses it high and it glides down perfectly in a soft breeze. Not so much as a crease or wrinkle shows. Then, she reaches into the basket and pulls things out one at a time, holding each item up like a game show hostess.

"Turkey with Swiss, light mayo. And I brought some Dijon mustard in case you're in the mood for that special sauce you love to whip up."

I nod and smirk. I know how hard she's trying but it's the best I can do.

"Fruit. It's all really ripe and fresh. Melon. Pineapple. Grapes. Small slices of apple, peach and pear. The slices are long and thin the way you like it."

Another nod, another smirk. I really am trying to smile, but my facial muscles won't cooperate.

"To drink I have iced tea, lemonade, and..." she slowly reaches into the basket then pulls out a bottle. "Merlot. Your favorite."

"Thanks, but I'm driving."

"Oh, stop it. One glass with lunch won't kill you."

Again, I nod.

"And for dessert, rice pudding."

I love rice pudding, especially Heidi's homemade rice pudding. I smile, and this time it's genuine. "That looks great, Heidi. Thank you."

"Of course. It's my pleasure."

We eat the meal in silence. There is nothing else to say. She tries to make eye contact once or twice, but I quickly look away. When I finish, I smile but can't find the words to thank her. She doesn't seem to mind. She reaches over to kiss me on the cheek, but I stand up before she gets the chance.

"Bye, Heidi. See you next year."

"I'll be here," she says, and I know she means it.

*　　*　　*

A man has certain expectations for his life. These expectations become more than just potential hopes and dreams. They become our essence. These expectations consume us. They make us what we are…and what we're not.

I stare up at the ceiling of my studio apartment, arms clasped over my head as if about to do a sit up – ignoring the neighbor in 2G who's yelling at the Chinese delivery guy – thinking about these very expectations. Not hope for the future, but the expectations I once had.

"You say white rice. Says right here."

"Fried rice. I asked for fried rice! The girl on the phone can't speak fuckin' English."

When I close my eyes, there are always three people in my mind's eye. Jack Maddox is a husband. Jack Maddox is a father. Jack Maddox owns a house in the suburbs, mowing his own lawn even though he could easily afford a gardener. Jack Maddox is wealthy and attractive. Jack Maddox sees beautiful women every day of his life and never pays them any mind. Jessica is the only woman for Jack Maddox.

"Fine! I come back with your fried rice!"

I open my eyes, and all of those things are gone. Jack Maddox no longer is a husband. Jessica is dead. Jack Maddox no longer is a father. Emily is dead. Jack Maddox no longer owns a house in the suburbs.

I roll off the bed and walk towards the window, stepping over the pizza boxes and ignoring the piled up dishes in the sink. Through the metal security grate I see the Chinese kid mutter to himself then hop on his bike and pedal towards Foo Chow on Second Avenue.

So, who is Jack Maddox if not those things?

Jack Maddox is dead. He died ten years ago. Jack Maddox is

buried in a field on Cherry Hill Road just off Route 9 in Brattleboro. I am what's left.

* * *

There's a light snow falling as I park my car in front of the telephone pole. I walk past the *Private Property* sign and my shoes sink into the fresh snow.

"Hi, Jack," Heidi says with that pretty smile. She is a year older than the last time I saw her, but her beauty has not diminished in the slightest. I want to tell her that, but I can't find the words. And I guess, on some level, I'm afraid she'll misinterpret what I mean.

I keep that to myself and simply nod and say, "Hi, Heidi." We embrace, and she tries to kiss me but I turn to the side. Her lips hit my neck. It tickles, slightly, but I don't laugh.

She does laugh, perhaps out of embarrassment. Hearing the familiar perky giggle forces me to turn towards her. Her hazel eyes are so striking. Her lips are thin but not too thin. She is a beautiful woman. She is my wife's sister. My wife's twin sister.

"I brought all your favorites again this year."

"Thank you."

We eat in silence, like we do every year. But this time, just as she unwraps the tinfoil from the bowl of rice pudding she says softly, "Jack?"

"Yes."

"It's been eleven years."

"I know."

"You're still a young man."

"I suppose."

"Jack, I just can't stand to see you like this."

"Like what?"

She pauses and as much as I don't want to, I look directly into her pretty hazels. She is every bit as beautiful as Jessica. If I close my eyes, I can almost fool myself into thinking she is Jessica. I shut my eyes and inhale. They wear the same perfume, and use the same shampoo. With my eyes closed, I can almost make myself believe it's her.

Until she says, "One day you need to get over her."

"What did you just say?"

She grabs my shoulders as if about to shake me and says, "You need to move on with your life, Jack. You need to move on. It's natural."

For an instant, I get angry. My impulse is to smack her arms right off of my shoulders. But I pause, and take in a heavy breath of *Honey* brand perfume and that shampoo with the kangaroo on the bottle. How can I be mad?

"I can never move on." I stand up and start walking slowly towards my car.

"Jack!" she says in a frantic tone filled with crackling phlegm. I turn and she outstretches her arm and says, "Your rice pudding. Don't forget the rice pudding. I made it just the way you like it."

I nod and smirk, then take the bowl from her and say, "I'll bring the bowl back next year."

"Keep it. I have plenty of bowls."

* * *

Every man needs certain delusions to survive. Some deny it. Others simply choose to call it something else: a daydream; a fantasy. But in reality, we know they are delusions. They are things that aren't true or real but we cling to them in order to survive. Kids have the Easter Bunny and Santa Claus, adults have God. I have the field on Cherry Hill Road.

It was in that field that I found my wife and child murdered. It was there that I first realized things could never be the same.

That I could never be the same.

I eat the rice pudding directly from the oversized bowl, slowly and deliberately. Then, I pull out my scrapbook. I look through it just once a year even though I carry it with me everywhere, sort of like a security blanket. After I get home from the picnic, I look through the album. It's a routine that I need in order to get through the next three hundred and sixty-four days and twenty hours without blowing my brains out. I often fantasize of suicide but know I'd never really do it. It wouldn't be right. Jessica and Emily were taken before their time, how can I voluntarily end mine? It just seems an injustice to them.

The scrapbook has pictures – lots of pictures. Me and Jessica. Jessica and Emily. Me and Emily. Jessica, me and Emily. Birthdays. Anniversaries. Mother's days. Father's days. I captured them all, and I treasure these pictures.

The last page of my scrapbook is a newspaper clipping. It is the only thing in the album that doesn't make me smile. Yet I must look at it every year. Once a year I review the entire scrapbook. It is part of my routine.

The headline reads: *Valentine's Day Massacre in Vermont: Father finds bodies of murdered kin.*

The article goes something like this, I've scratched out the names because it's too painful to read them:

A wealthy Westchester businessman found the mutilated bodies of his wife and daughter in a field in a rural area of Brattleboro. <illegible>, age thirty and <illegible>, age three were raped, brutally sliced then their bodies were dumped in a field. "We have no suspects at this time," Sheriff Ronald F. Hartman told reporters, "However we have several leads and are vehemently investigating each one."

I stop reading there. I always stop reading there. Anyone who reads the newspaper knows that all the important stuff is in the first paragraph. I have the entire article clipped, but I never read past the first paragraph. It is part of my annual routine.

*   *   *

"Tough ride up?" Heidi asks.

"Yeah, hit a lot of traffic."

"Me too."

"Took me four and a half hours."

"Close to five for me," she says as she bites into her sandwich.

"You should have taken my short cut at Queechy Lake, saves a good fifteen minutes."

She nods, takes a sip of Merlot, then says meekly, "Jack?"

"What is it?" I snap. I hate to snap at her, but I just can't help it. The tone of her voice lets me know I'm not going to like what she's about to say.

"Jack, how come we never speak?"

"Nothing to say."

"How come we never meet more than once a year?"

"Once a year I visit. I like having you as company. But if it's too much trouble…"

She cuts me off and says, "It's no trouble. But what I mean is, we live less than twenty blocks from one another, and the only time we meet is here. Can't we meet on nicer terms?"

"I don't think so."

She sighs loudly and says, "How about now, can we talk now?"

"Sure."

"I'll talk. You never ask me about my life."

I realize how selfish that must seem to her. The last thing I mean to be is selfish where Heidi is concerned. She is without a doubt the nicest, most unselfish person I've ever met.

"Okay, Heidi. Tell me something about your life."

"Ask me something. What do you want to know?"

"Where do you work these days? Still a paralegal for Himmelfarb and Schier?"

"No! Don't be silly. I graduated law school years ago."

I laugh, then scratch my head and say, "You're right. I'm sorry I never take an interest in your life. I just get preoccupied sometimes."

"I know. I understand. Ask me something else."

"Do you have a boyfriend?" It's a natural question, but as soon as I ask it, I wish I could take it back.

"No."

"Not lately?"

"No. Not ever."

"Never? Come on, Heidi. You're a beautiful woman. Talented and smart. Well off. There must be tons of guys asking you out."

"There have been a few. But I always say no."

"How come?"

Very quietly, almost inaudibly, she says, "Because my heart belongs to someone already."

I look down at the picnic basket, then reach over for the bottle of wine. I take a long swig right from the bottle and ask, "Do you believe in love at first sight, Heidi?"

She shrugs. "I suppose."

"I fell in love with your sister the very first day I met her."

"Really?" she says, now smiling that great smile as her voice perks up. "That blind date that Jenny McGrath fixed you two up on!"

"Absolutely. From day one I knew she was the only girl for me."

"Man. That was so long ago. You two were just kids. You couldn't have been thinking about marriage at that age."

"Not in that sense. But still, I knew. It's weird. I mean, you know me, I am the least spiritual guy there is, even before all this happened. But when I first saw your sister in that black and pink polka-dotted shirt…I knew."

"Oh my god! That shirt. I remember that shirt."

"So do I. I'll never forget that shirt."

We smile at each other and finish our meal. The rice pudding is just as tasty as ever.

✴ ✴ ✴

Being alone in a big house is unbearable. I'll never forget when I bought my house. I expected to live there forever, but once I was all alone, it was too big. I wanted something small. Something that would look full. I don't really like it, but I stay here anyway. I doubt I'll ever move.

It's noisy, but I like it that way. There's a baby crying. The neighbors upstairs are shuffling around, as usual. The guy next door is yelling at the pizza delivery guy.

"I said no anchovies!"

"Sir, you specifically asked for anchovies."

"No you dipshit! I specifically said no anchovies."

"Alright. Alright. Take it easy. I'll go get you another pie."

"Hurry up, man. I'm hungry."

It might sound silly, but I enjoy listening to my neighbor holler at the deliver guy every night. It reminds me that I'm still on planet Earth. My neighbor is great for keeping my focus on the present.

I walk past the mirror, ignoring the straggly-haired, unshaved man in it, and yell into the security grate of my opened window, "2G, keep it down." We've been neighbors for a decade, and I've never learned his name, nor he mine. "I'm trying to get some work done."

"Hey, fuck you!" he yells back, then punches his side of the wall that separates our apartments.

I open the grate, stick my head out the window and yell, "Knock it off. You're gonna break your hand, man."

He sticks his head out and says in a surprisingly calm tone, "I'll break my hand any time I goddamn please. Okay?"

I throw up my hand in mock surrender and say, "Fine. Just keep it down a little. Please."

He nods his pudgy face while blowing a lip-fart. I really don't care if he quiets down or not, I just felt like arguing with him.

The calendar that hangs from my wall reads *February 4.* Better take my suit to the cleaners and make an appointment at the barbershop.

* * *

"The sky is really gray," she says. "Sure looks like snow."

"They're forecasting a blizzard."

"I brought all your favorites again this year, Jack."

"Great!"

"I have something extra special this year, Jack." I'm fully expecting homemade rice pudding, but instead she pulls off her sweatshirt to reveal a black and pink polka-dotted shirt. One I haven't seen in about twenty years.

"Wow. That's the shirt," I say, sort of dumbfounded but not sad at all.

"You recognize it?"

"Of course I do. It's the shirt Jessica wore the day we met. The day I fell in love with her."

"It's the shirt, alright and it still fits."

I smile at that. She really is just as thin as she was twenty years ago.

"But the shirt isn't Jessica's. It's mine."

"What, did she borrow it that day?"

"Nope." She's looking at me in a way I've never seen before. I thought I knew every mannerism and every facial tick Heidi had. But she is looking at me in a way that she never has before. "I wore the shirt that day."

"What?"

"Your first date, Jack. It was with me."

"What are you talking about?"

"Jessica came down with the flu the day before your date. She begged me to fill in for her. Jenny said such good things about you and she didn't want to blow it. So, I filled in."

I scratch my head, trying to digest what I'm being told.

"It was only that one time, you see. You couldn't tell us apart yet. You didn't know us."

"Why are you telling me this now?"

"Don't you see, Jack. You fell in love with me at first sight. You fell in love with Jess later, but that first date was me."

"It was you?"

"Yes."

"That was twenty years ago. It means nothing."

"It means everything. It means we have chemistry."

"No. It doesn't mean that."

She wraps her arms around me and pulls me close. I don't fight, but I don't exactly go along either. I just lean against her body, stiff as the telephone pole I can see over her shoulder slightly blurred by the crosswind of snow that's begun to fall.

"I fell in love that day, too, Jack. I, too, believe in love at first sight. I couldn't hurt my sister, but I always secretly regretted it."

"Regretted what?"

"Not getting the chance to be with you myself."

"I'm sorry, Heidi. But it's too late."

"No. It isn't. We're right for each other. Jessica would understand. She would give her blessing. I know she would."

"I can't give my blessing."

"Please, Jack. It's time to move on with your life."

"My wife and child were murdered. I can never forget that."

Heidi shakes her head, back and forth, back and forth, back and forth again. Her hands go to her face as she starts to sob loudly. For the first time, she looks ugly to me.

"No," she whispers.

"They were murdered. I killed them."

"That's not true," she says just bawling like a schoolgirl.

I get up and wipe the sweat from my forehead, then start towards my car. She picks up her things and quickly follows me.

When I get to Cherry Hill Road, my car is right where I left it. Parked next to the pole.

"Why did I take this goddamned short cut?" I ask, without turning around to face her.

"You have to move on with your life."

"The fucking Elmo tape blasting! The kid screaming, and Jessica yelling at me to slow down! I got distracted."

"Please, Jack. Stop torturing yourself."

"It was dark. I was tired. But I had to keep my precious four-hour schedule."

"It's over, Jack. You have to let it go."

I turn to face her, the bowl of rice pudding trembling in her hand.

"It was an accident," she whispers.

"I killed them."

I open the car door and step inside, then roll down the window. She hands me the bowl with the rice pudding.

"I'll bring the bowl back next year."

"Keep it. I don't want to have anymore picnics in the snow."

I start my engine and pull around the pole, ignoring the burgundy paint stains. My scrapbook sits in the passenger seat, and I open it to the last page while gunning my engine. There is a picture of a family I don't recognize. My tires skid against the icy gravel. I pull the clipping from the book, crumple it and toss it out into the fresh snow.

Old Maid Syndrome

'No! She didn't!" I giggled with unmasked joy.

"She did! She did! Sara got engaged," Chrissy laughed in her trademark mousy tone.

"I can't believe it, this is soooooo exciting," I said, tossing my brown curly hair. I could barely hold the princess phone between my fingernails, my hands were so shaky. "Shit! I think I chipped a nail!"

"Calm down, calm down."

"'kay."

"Guess who's the maid of honor."

"Oh my God, she asked you?"

"Of course, we've only been best friends for twenty years, if she didn't ask me I'd never forgive her."

"That's so cool, Chris."

"And guess who else is gonna be asked to be in the wedding party."

I knew Chris meant me, but I had to hear it to be sure. "Who?" I asked, straining to hold back the giggles.

"You Evelyn, of course she's gonna ask you."

"THAT IS WONDERFUL!!!!" I hollered. "I can't believe this. Sara is getting married."

After the initial giddiness started to lessen, I admit, a little jealousy kicked in. I just couldn't help it. Chrissy sensed it and the laughter faded.

"What is it, Ev? You're so quiet all of a sudden," Chrissy asked softly.

"Nothing, nothing," I insisted. Not that there was any point to bullshitting Chris.

"Don't tell me nothing, sweetie, we've been friends too long for that."

"You know, it's just that Sara is four years younger than me."

"So, she's two years younger than me, and I'm not married."

"Yeah but you've been with Freddie for three years. It's just a matter of time for you two. Me, I've got no one but Saki to keep me company."

"So, Saki is a good friend," Chrissy said with a semi-sincere laugh.

"Yeah, Saki's great," I mumbled, as my golden retriever ran over upon hearing his name, "but he ain't gonna replace my vibrator anytime soon, you know what I mean, honey." Saki put his head in my lap, and I stroked his furry head while he wagged his tail.

"I sure hope not, that would be way-weird!"

"I'm just really afraid, Chris."

"Afraid? Afraid of what?"

"Well, when I was twenty, I was hot. At twenty-five, I was a knockout. But now, well, you know."

"No, I don't know. You're still beautiful. Any guy would be lucky to have you. Any guy."

"Yeah, but that P.P. is kicking in."

"Come off it, you're thin as can be, so I don't want to hear shit about 'Porker Potential.'"

"I guess I'm okay, for thirty-four. But my ass is a little flabbier than it used to be. And I stopped wearing belly shirts years ago."

"Would you stop it, Ev. You are still a hottie. And thirty-four is not old. Not even close."

"I guess."

"I don't guess, I know."

"There's something more. It's not just the couple extra pounds on the scale. It's…"

"What honey? What is it?"

"The bottom line is…well…it's…"

"Come on, Ev, you can talk to me."

"I don't want to grow old alone."

"I know honey, but things will change for you. Don't give up hope."

* * *

Planning and celebrating led to dress fitting, then before I had time to feel sorry for myself, the wedding day was upon us. Riding in the limousine, I was all smiles. After all, I had so much to be happy about. As the white Lincoln stretch began the two-mile journey of transporting the wedding party to the reception hall, we all looked out the window, cackling a happy cackle. We were unabashed at times like these. Who cared if we looked ditzy to the farty old driver?

"Who was that guy?" I asked.

"Which guy?" Chris responded without any attempts to mask her excitement.

"You know, the tall guy with long dark hair in the wedding party."

"Ohhhhh, that guy. I always knew you had good taste."

"Well, who is he?"

"I think he's Johnny's cousin. Do you wanna meet him?" she asked playfully.

"Yes, I want to meet him!"

"When we get to the hall I'll see if I can work some magic."

"You better be subtle about it, or I'll kill you, Chris."

"Of course I will. I'll tell him that you're horny, desperate and lonely."

"Shut up you bitch!" I giggled as I lightly punched Chrissy's shoulder. I think I was turning red. She just loved to embarrass me.

"I'll drop a little hint to Johnny that you think his cousin is cute."

"Yeah right, you're gonna make me look stupid."

"No I won't! Don't you have any faith in me?"

Chris was talking to me, but I wasn't looking at her. I was looking outside at the next car. One of the other limousines, the one holding the groomsman, was passing on the left.

"He's so hot!" Chris laughed. "If you don't go after him I might."

"Chris, you're terrible, you have a man."

"I'm kidding!"

We stopped talking, and all the girls turned towards the other car and gazed at the guy. He turned and looked over, and the car filled with laughter.

"Oh my god, I am soooo mortified!" I shouted, dropping my face into my hands.

"Stop it, why?"

"He saw me staring. I'm so humiliated."

"Stop overreacting, we were all staring."

Sara's younger sister, Hillary, turned to her girlfriend and said, "He seems arrogant. He knows he's good-looking."

The friend nodded, then said, "Did you see how he flipped his long hair like a girl?"

"How do you know he's arrogant?" I asked, although they weren't talking to me directly.

"Oh, I don't know. It's just a cocky look he gave us. The way he twirled his goatee. You didn't notice, Evelyn?"

"No!" I said and turned my back on the other girls.

✴   ✴   ✴

As soon as there was a break at the reception, Chris wasted no time. She worked her magic, and they came over towards me. I was so tingly!

"This is my cousin, Emmanuel," Johnny said with a smile, then a wink in my direction.

"Hello, Evelyn," Emmanuel said in a soothing, low tone.

Emmanuel extended his hand and when I touched it, I think I melted. He was so warm and firm, yet gentle at the same time. He kissed the top of my palm lightly, without puckering or leaving any wetness. Me on the other hand felt moisture between my legs and under my arms instantly.

"Shall we dance?" he asked. But I was too dazed to answer. Ever the gentleman, he said, "Perhaps you'd rather take a seat."

"Uh, sure," I said, without taking my eyes from his – they were almost magically hypnotic, and a sharp shade of hazel.

Emmanuel led me to his table and pulled out a chair for me to sit in. I followed his lead, and sat. Finally taking my eyes off of his, I noticed Chrissy looking over with a wide smile. Chrissy waved quickly – that rapid circular wave of hers – then turned away nonchalantly.

We talked and laughed. Conversation came so easily and flowed so naturally. There never seemed to be an uncomfortable pause. We danced, a long and slow dance. The day flew by and I admit…I was entranced. When it came time to catch the bouquet, it sailed into my hands; I didn't even lunge or jump, it just came right to me as if shot out of Cupid's bow.

Emmanuel slid the garter up my leg, very softly and slowly, yet he didn't seem embarrassed. Me, on the other hand, I was beet red once he finally reached his destination with the lacey belt.

"HIGHER! Go higher!" Chrissy called with glee. That bitch! I told you she loved embarrassing me.

"THAT'S HIGH ENOUGH!" I shouted as the room laughed. It was high enough for a public display anyway! Once in private I knew it would be different though. There wouldn't be any limits put on him in private. How could I? I was in love. Just that quickly, and I was sure he felt it too.

He was perfect! Good looking. Good job. Never been married before. No kids. No ex-wife. No baggage. I just couldn't believe it. It was the best night of my life. The man of my dreams had finally arrived!

Emmanuel led me outside, and called a cab. Nobody complained that I snuck off early. They were all too happy for me. He opened the door, helped me in, and got in beside me. We cuddled the entire ride to his place. He never made any moves, didn't even try to kiss me. Just held me close, firmly yet nicely. The butterflies in my belly were whipping around. My palms were wet and tingly. I was lightheaded.

Emmanuel helped me out of the taxi. There was a small puddle of muddy water in the gutter. Before I had the chance to panic over my apricot dress, he lifted me up and over it – I flew into his arms – then placed me back down. I felt secure in his grasp. He wasn't overly muscular, but he seemed so sturdy, until he put me back down. He stumbled a bit, and his face grimaced.

"Are you okay?" I asked.

"Fine. Of course, I'm fine."

"Not too heavy, I hope," I said with a sheepish smile.

"Don't be silly. Just got a little woozy for a second. Had nothing to do with you."

We walked arm in arm into the building. The doorman quickly opened the door and held it for us, then dutifully jogged by us, over to the elevator, and pushed the 'up' button.

"Thanks, Charles," Emmanuel said and smiled.

"Of course, Mr. Appel. You and the lady enjoy your evening."

"Oh, we will," I said with a giddy giggle. I guess I should have felt a little trashy under the circumstances. Normally, I would have. I never slept with a guy on the first date, ever. In thirty-four years. But I didn't feel cheap. Not in the slightest. This was perfect. Anyway, I'm sure Charles didn't mean it that way. He was just being polite.

We got off the elevator on the top floor. There was only one door. His apartment took up the entire floor! Once inside, I could see that it was something else! A huge fish tank covered the entire foyer wall. Orange, red and yellow tropical fish swam around happily. Art covered the walls; I'm sure it was rare and expensive too, but what do I know about art? The couch was big and cushy, and next to it was a fireplace.

"Wow! A fireplace. Can we light it? Please, please, please!"

"Of course."

Emmanuel flicked a switch, and the flames shot right up. The warmth and brightness was both alarming and beautiful.

"Wow. This apartment is amazing, Emmanuel. I've never been in a place quite like it."

"Relax, Evelyn. My home is yours. Would you like a drink?"

"Sure."

"Booze? Wine? What would you like?" he asked as he gracefully glided along the hardwood floor like a cross-country skier. He stopped at the long oak bar and pulled out two glasses.

"Oh, whatever you're having." I wasn't much of a drinker, and I couldn't think straight enough to choose something.

"Wine then. Red wine."

"Excellent, Emmanuel. Red wine would be excellent."

Emmanuel carried over the two glasses. I sipped lightly first, as he gulped. Then I gulped too. It was very sweet, and it went right to my already tipsy head.

"More?" he asked.

"Not for me."

"Okay, I'll just have one more."

As he walked back towards the bar, I turned to the fire. It burned brightly, and the wood crackled. He was quiet, and I was quiet. Just the sound of burning wood crackling, and a soft pouring of wine in the background. It was perfect. I had my share of failed romances as an adult, and plenty of backseat debacles in my teens. Truthfully, I hadn't had good sex with anyone but my vibrator...ever. Tonight would be different. It was just too perfect. And it couldn't get anything but better.

Emmanuel walked back, sipping the wine. The glass was empty by the time he reached the couch, and he placed the goblet down on the glass coffee table. He gently slipped off my heels. I'm not sure why I hadn't kicked them off already myself. But it was as if I needed him to do everything for me. He parted my legs with the grace of a swan cutting a light wake into a clear pond and then slid my stockings down. I never met a man like this. There wasn't a rough bone in his body. My dress slipped down as if he didn't even touch it. My strapless push-up slid off like a figure skater on fresh, smooth ice. Then, Emmanuel peeled my panties off.

He dropped his pants and slipped out of his own shirt and cumberbund. Then he disappeared, down into the couch, and into my crotch. The fluffy couch absorbed his head, and I couldn't even see it. But boy could I feel it. The way he moved his tongue around in rhythmic circles was incredible. It was going in and out of me while his fingers gently rubbed my clit. I was instantly lost, and lost completely. I arched my back, and leaned my head all the way back, stretching and straining uncontrollably. Emmanuel was making these quiet grunts as he worked me, which only added to my excitement. I was usually too inhibited to make noise with a man, but I grunted back at him, he had me feeling so comfortable and relaxed.

The pleasurable tension built up and built up as Emmanuel rubbed and licked. He sucked my lips gently away from my body, and his tongue and fingers entered my insides, then caressed the outsides. It just kept building up and building up inside of me, the friction getting harder and harder, yet just the right amount. I was wet enough to handle it at this point, and he sensed it, picking up his pace with his tongue and rubbing the top of my lips faster and faster. I kept arching my back further and further, stretching myself at the seams as I quivered and shook. I gripped the pillows and twisted. Just when I thought I'd go crazy from it, when the passion was so fucking intense that I was going to either orgasm or die, at just that moment when I was about to holler, "I can't take it any more! STOP! This is too fucking good, Emmanuel!" finally, I came. I'm sure I screamed from the unbridled passion, although how can I even remember? I was so lost in the moment. I had cum before from my vibrator, and once or twice with a man, but never, ever was I so free that I could shriek like a horny banshee unleashed from a thirty-four-year-old crypt of bad sex. I was always too damned uptight. But not with Emmanuel. He was a pro at oral. And more importantly, he was a pro at making me feel special.

When he came up from the couch, he smiled, and I smiled back. Then he lay down, and took me on him. He didn't ask, and I didn't object. I just wound up on top of him and he lay back, bouncing me up and down like I was his plaything. And I loved it. The sex didn't last long, but at that point, who cared? I could see he was tired, and so was I. He was breathing so heavily and sucking wind that I was alarmed for a second, but he smiled his calming smile, and I fell asleep in his arms, right there on the couch.

I woke up the next morning and smelled coffee. *He even makes coffee!* I still couldn't find a single fault in Emmanuel. He walked over to me very slowly. He was smiling, but looked a little weather-beaten. I guess that wasn't strange, he hadn't showered or anything.

"Evelyn," he handed me a mug of coffee and looked me right in the eye – those powerful hazels just grabbed me.

"Hi, honey. Last night was wonderful."

"Yes, it was."

"It was the best night of my life. Ever!"

"I'm so happy that I can please you."

"Oh, you do. You do!"

"I want to make you happy, forever. For the rest of your life, Evelyn."

"Emmanuel, what are you saying?"

"I'm saying I want to marry you."

"Are you serious?"

"Of course. I want you to marry me."

I was stunned, and speechless. All I could do was stare into those big eyes, and he looked back, never once breaking eye contact.

Emmanuel took my hand firmly, put my coffee mug down, dropped to one knee, and asked, "Evelyn, will you marry me?"

I held his glare, just waiting for him to crack a smile, or laugh. Or tell me he was kidding. It was all so fast, and we just met. But my heart told me this was it. I'd waited thirty-four years, and finally I knew: I wouldn't grow old alone!

"Yes, Emmanuel. YES! Of course I'll marry you." I grabbed Emmanuel and hugged him, the tightest firmest hug I'd ever hugged. Tears of joy watered my eyes.

Emmanuel continued to smile at me, and his eyes stayed on me. Then his expression changed, and he looked away. He stumbled, and quickly sat down.

"What is it, honey? What's wrong?" I asked.

"I'm sorry, Evelyn. I'm feeling weak."

"Is everything okay?" I jumped up and ran to the bar, filled a glass with water and ran it back to him. "Drink honey, you'll feel better."

Emmanuel slugged the water down quickly, and turned to me. "More please," he said as he handed me the glass.

I ran back to the bar and refilled the glass. As I walked it back I asked, "Are you sure you're okay?"

"Evelyn, there's something that you must know about me, before our relationship goes any further."

"Of course. Tell me, honey."

"I have a rare condition. A very rare kidney ailment."

"Oh my god! That's so awful."

"It is. It is. It makes me very weak at times, and my stamina is effected."

"Well, have you seen a doctor?"

"A doctor," he said with a chuckle. "I've been to all the best doctors in the country. They can't do anything for me."

"They can't?"

"All we can do is wait. I need a new kidney. And there is a long waiting list for kidneys."

"Well, I'll give you one of mine."

"Oh, Evelyn, that is so nice of you. It's too nice of you."

"Nonsense. We are going to spend our lives together. And I want yours to be a long and healthy one."

"There are risks. To me, but also to you."

"Emmanuel, I will risk everything. I need you to be healthy."

We went to see Dr. Rothman the very next day. The tests went beautifully. It appeared that my kidney would be compatible with his body. I insisted that we schedule the surgery as soon as possible. To hell with ring shopping (oh my god, did I really say that?!). So just a few days later, less than a week after I'd met Emmanuel, I was giving him my kidney.

✶ ✶ ✶

I awoke in a lot of pain. I looked down, pulled back my gown, and twisted around, trying hard not to stretch the I.V. line in my arm. There was a huge scar in my side where they'd cut me open. And the scabs around it were gross! They were full of pus. They didn't look right. I immediately buzzed for the nurse. She came, along with the doctor.

"Evelyn, I need you to relax," Dr. Rothman said.

"I'm in a lot of pain, doctor."

"I'm sure you are. There's a nasty infection. We are giving you strong doses of anti-biotics to fight it off. Don't worry."

"Emmanuel?"

"He's doing great, Evelyn. Just great."

"Can I see him?"

"Sure. But you need to stay in bed."

"Well, can I call his room?"

"Actually, he's gone home. I've told him to make sure he gets extra rest and takes all his medications. But otherwise, he should be in great shape."

"Oh."

Emmanuel was home already. It was great news, of course.

But if I was still here, shouldn't he come see me?

I picked up the phone and called his number. There was no answer. He was probably too tired. Just following orders and getting rest.

As the infection spread all over my insides, I spent weeks in and out of consciousness. They had me doped up on all kinds of shit. At times, I forgot where I was. If anyone came to visit, I guess I was too groggy to notice. But daily, I called Emmanuel. I had to know how he was. He just didn't answer. I called, and called. Finally, I realized he must need me. It was the only explanation.

My need to save him gave me strength. Even though it hurt to stand, I stood. I yanked the I.V. needle out of my arm, and looked for my shoes. I didn't bother to dress. I hadn't eaten solid food in weeks, but I managed to walk all the way home. My love for Emmanuel carried me.

I opened the door, and Saki rushed me. He was so happy to see me, and I him.

"You poor thing? You're emaciated." I looked in the hallway mirror and noticed, I was too. I fed Saki, and ate what little I could stomach myself. Then, I showered and did my best to make myself pretty for him. My shaky hands ran my make-up a bit, but I did my very best. Emmanuel would appreciate the effort. When I walked out, Saki followed behind.

I limped all the way uptown to Emmanuel's palace. When I got there, I saw Charles out front, pulling opened the door to a large limousine. I was about to call and say hello to Charles when I saw Emmanuel getting out of the car, and with him was a familiar, pretty face. It was Chrissy. That fucking bitch. She didn't come and visit me once in the hospital. And now, she was with him! They were arm in arm – all over each other! Groping like a couple of hormone-filled teenagers.

They walked inside without looking in my direction, and Saki and I walked up to the front door. I was sure Charles would turn me away, he was so damn thorough at his job. But just as we got to the front, a woman in white fur walked out with her pathetically well-groomed white poodle – they matched. Saki ran at the poodle, and yanked the leash right out of my hands. The woman screamed and Charles ran over to her aid. I walked inside, unseen.

When I got up to the penthouse, I was pretty sure the door would be opened. I was right. I guess when you have the only apartment on the floor, why bother locking it. I wouldn't know that kind of arrogance, or affluence. But whatever.

I walked inside and stood in the foyer. I didn't have to walk all the way in to see what was going on. The fish tank wall was easy to see through, although the apartment was dimly lit. Emmanuel lit candles and the two sat on the couch. The fireplace burned. Chrissy was giggling her typical, ditsy giggle. I used to think it was cute. That phony!

I watched them sip wine, and Emmanuel did most of the talking. I couldn't hear them through the thick fish tank's glass, other than that bitch's cackling; goddamn did that cut through walls! The two of them began undressing each other slowly, then the mood changed.

Emmanuel ripped her bra off, and Chrissy bit his neck. He yanked her from the back of her panties and carried her into the bedroom like she was his lunchbox. I could see her legs kicking wildly in midair, and I heard that obnoxious giggling, along with, "Oh, Emmanuel, you're so rough." Where did he find this new-found strength? From my fucking kidney that ingrate!

They disappeared down a long corridor, and I began riffling through drawers. I found a scissors. I rubbed it against my arm lightly, and it was sharp. Perfect. I'd cut that bastard's dick right off! And her tits too, while I was at it!

I walked slowly down the corridor, it twisted and turned and there were many rooms along the way: a study, a library, and a playroom with a pool table and such. What a place! I'd never seen it all before. I'd have gotten lost for sure, but I just followed the giggles. It wasn't too hard.

As the giggles got louder, my pace slowed. I was so weak. I stopped and held the wall for balance. Just then I heard, "Fuck me, Emmanuel. Fuck me harder!" and my equilibrium came right back. I walked around one more bend and there they were. What made her so special that she got to see the bedroom? I never did!

Chrissy was yelling and cackling, bouncing up and down on top of him.

"Ooooo, Freddie never fucks like this."

What a horrible thing to say. Freddie devoted his whole fucking world to her! Doted over her every movement. Treated her like a queen!

She hopped up and down, and then he yanked her off, and tossed her down. He flipped her over, bent her hips, grabbed her ass, and put it up in the air.

Whack!

Emmanuel spanked her tiny little ass. Yeah, fine, so Chrissy did have a killer body.

"Ouch!" she shot back, but it didn't hurt.

Whack! Whack!

He pounded her ass again, then again.

"Oooo."

"You like?" he asked in this evil tone of voice.

"Is that the hardest you can hit?"

Wham! He really nailed her, and she clearly loved it.

He started fucking her doggy, wildly. His ass was flying 'round and 'round, as if he was waving it at my face. He was groaning this pathetic groan, making these noises. What a retard! What did I ever see in him? I can't believe I fell for his bullshit Casanova act. Look at what a bully he could be, when he had the energy. She was banging into the wall, and loving it. When he did me, it was like thirty seconds and done. He'd been slamming her around for five minutes already, and showing no signs of slowing.

His balls were slapping around, and I was staring at them, transfixed. I looked at the sharp metal scissors, then at his balls. I entered the room and walked towards them.

"Fuck me, Emmanuel! Fuck me hard!"

And boy was he; she was whacking into the wall, and this grandiose wood headboard and not caring at all. How did she plan to explain those bumps to Freddie? He'd believe whatever bullshit she told him, he was so whipped.

"Harder! Fuck me harder."

"Uh! Uh!" Emmanuel grunted loudly, followed by these soft, goofy little, "ew, ew," noises.

Mix her yelling, with his groaning, throw in her giggling with the sound of her head smashing that wooden post and goddamn was this something else. His ass was staring at me, thrashing around in circles, and forwards and backwards. On and on. It was the never-ending fuck from hell.

"Fuck me! Fuck me you beast!"

"Uh! Uh!"

"Fuck me harder you bastard! Yank my hair! Spank my ass! Come on you wussy boy, fuck me harder!"

"Ew, ew."

That ass was still laughing at me, and I was right behind them. It amazed me that he couldn't feel my breath on his back, or hear me, as I was breathing just as heavily as they were. But those two were oblivious. It just kept on, even as I raised the scissors up over my head.

"Fuck me harder! Harder you wussy boy. Come on, rich man, can't you fuck a girl any harder?"

"Uh, uh. Ew, ew."

Finally, I just couldn't take another second of listening to his thighs slapping her ass. I brought down the scissors, right into his back, and twisted.

"Ahhhhhhhhhh!" he yelled out.

I used what little strength I had left to open the scissors and tear away the flesh. I twisted it around and around, just like his ass had been twisting for the last ten minutes. I ripped a hole wide open in him. I don't know how long it took, but the stupid, spoiled rich boy did nothing but moan. You'd think his reflexes would kick in and he'd either fight back or try and weasel away. But he just squeezed her hips and hollered.

I reached into his insides, and yelled, "Give me back my kidney you ungrateful prick!"

"Oh my god!" Chrissy yelled from underneath.

He passed out, and all of his weight came down on top of her. The poor little petite thing was pinned. But she managed to twist around to look up at me.

I yanked out my kidney, cutting away at the veins and muscle connecting it to him. There was still a little of his tissue left, so I bit it off, and spit it right in her face. I dropped the scissors, took my kidney, and left.

EXPRESS DELIVERY

Martin looked at the foot sitting nakedly in the box in front of him with a numbness that only true terror can inspire. All he could picture in his head was the way he had smiled at the boy from Express Delivery. He had smiled and thanked him whilst taking possession of the innocuous looking brown box with the blue and red company logo down the side. The logo down the side, and his left foot sitting cosily within. And there was no doubt about it; that was definitely his left foot. The only difference between the one in the box and the one inside his slipper was that the one in the package wasn't attached to the rest of him. Oh yes, and the one inside that padded tartan warmness didn't have a tag tied round its big toe stating in bold black letters:

YOU HAVE TWO DAYS.

Even though he'd recognised the landscape and the structure of the foot immediately when he'd seen it, he still pulled off his slipper in the vain hope that the foot had been delivered to the wrong door, that there was someone else in the world that had gotten themselves into some deep shit, and this was just a crazy coincidence. Being very careful not to touch the contents, he picked the box up from the coffee table and placed it on the floor. Feeling the heaviness and uneven weight of the package made the skin between his fingers tingle in disgust. Maybe it was time to put his toes on a diet, ha, ha. Not very funny, he concluded to himself. Not very funny at all.

Looking at the two together there was no doubt about it, they were definitely a pair. The same dark brown mole just inside the arch, and the same little tuft of hairs sprouting from his big toe. If he counted them he would bet his breakfast that there would be the same amount of hairs on each, and each one of those hairs would be identical to that of its counterpart. His mouth dried instantly, and although his face was flushing he could feel a chill running through his body as his blood pulled back into the centre of him, protecting itself.

He looked at the note again. YOU HAVE TWO DAYS. Shit, oh shit, oh shit. How had he let things get this far? Although dramatically delivered, the words themselves were pretty irrelevant. They were just a time scale, tickety tock said Mr. Clock, and all that jazz. The real message was the foot itself. It told him their intentions more fluently than any amount of words could attempt. The message was pretty simple.

In two days time, if he didn't produce the money, he was a dead man. A dead man, and yet not a dead man. He would cease to exist, be rubbed out, whacked or whatever these gangsters called their form of murder these days, but no one would find his body, no one would grieve for him and more importantly, there would be no police investigation, because, hey, to all intents and purposes he would still be alive. Not the original him naturally. No, he himself would be incinerated neatly out of society. Not him, but a perfect copy. The perfect clone that would visit his children at weekends, sleep in his bed, and wear his goddamned tartan slippers. The clone that would be found a job and would pay a percentage of its salary every month to its creators; partly to cover the cost of bringing it into the world and party to cover the debts of its dead predecessor. He was only thirty now, so that gave them a good thirty years to get a return on their money.

He stood up on shaky legs and crossed the room. Standing on tiptoes he reached over the top of the bureau, feeling the dust shifting beneath his fingertips. After a few seconds of blind fumbling, his hand found what it was looking for, and pulled down the small tin. Cigarettes had been illegal in England for over ten years, but thank the Lord for small mercies, the government wasn't as harsh about it as they were in the USA. Sure, you could get busted for it, but if you only had a few for personal use, the police tended to turn a blind eye. After all, most of those guys weren't beyond having the odd puff themselves. The end of the Marlboro blazed red as he sucked in deeply, the harshness of the stale tobacco tickling his throat, and as his head began to swim and buzz, he returned to sit on the sofa. Hell, he might even smoke two today. There was a time when the fear of getting busted for smoking would have kept him awake at nights wondering if the neighbours could smell his once a fortnight law-breaking activity, but those days were well and truly over.

He could feel his panic resurgent within him. *Two days.* Two days to find one hundred thousand pounds, or the clone had his life. He pulled harder on the cigarette, not wanting to waste any of its polluting cargo.

He had been expecting something, but not this. Cloning wasn't the big deal over here, not like in big brother's America, where the surge in the industry had created national paranoia. Was your mother really your mother, or has Dad traded her in for a replacement? For a price, you could have the satisfaction of murder with none of the comeback. There were even strong rumours in many leading international newspapers that the President hadn't really recovered from that heart attack he had last year, and this was in fact, version two, the new model. But here in little England, it had never really taken off. Or so he had thought until now.

It was common knowledge that the Greater London Mafia ran most of the city, and some said the country, but they must have way more money than he originally thought to spend out like this on a nobody like him. A whole load more money.

He could remember sitting in that huge office, with its leather chair, sweating against his trousers, wondering if when he stood up there would be a damp patch there betraying his nerves, his naiveté, his lack of criminal experience. He did not do things like this. He was a LAW ABIDING CITIZEN. He was a respected space-planning officer and he had PROSPECTS. The man who owned the illegally large office had just smiled and asked him the details of the program that he required, and then politely offered him a cup of tea. He imagined a solitary hair falling desperately slowly to the floor as he recalled leaning forward to take the delicate bone china cup. Whether it was a hair, or a flake of skin, it was irrelevant. They had got his DNA from somewhere.

He reluctantly extinguished the smouldering butt. This was all Carol's fault. If she hadn't told him out of the blue she didn't want him anymore, to leave her and the kids to get on with their own lives, to go and live with his precious work, then he wouldn't be in this situation. There would have been no Express Delivery. He smiled acidly to himself. It was easy for Carol, but then, everything had always been easy for Carol, the archetypal little rich kid who never *had* to work. Daddy had been the creator of the Space Management Council, after all. Revolutionising London's housing situation. Hero of the people, etc. etc. blah, blah, blah. The sharp bitterness in his head felt like it was scraping at his skull.

When they had first met he thought she had admired his ambition, his determination to get on, to succeed, to be SOME-ONE. She finally admitted, five years and two children later that all she really wanted him to be was her husband, her companion. Someone to spend all day at the tennis club with. They were never really what they had pretended to be for each other, and faking it wasn't working anymore. That's what she thought anyway. She never bothered to ask his opinion as she virtually shoved him out the door.

Deep inside though, he figured that she just got bored. Simple as that. Bored of her working class toy. Whatever it was, one day she just couldn't stand the sight of him anymore. But God did he love her, spoiled brat or not. Maybe he loved her almost as much as he hated her. It was always rather hard to tell with these things. Different moments, different moods. And these days he was finding it hard to tell if it was virtual Carol or biological Carol that still had the hold on him.

There was a spluttering sound from the box on the floor, and he watched as the foot mulched down into brown gel, folding in on itself from the inside, looking like an old-fashioned rubber veruca sock with no solidity within it, until the outer layer itself melted away, leaving only a damp lump of some glutinous substance behind. Revolting as it was to watch, he wasn't really surprised. A whole spare foot sent through the post could most definitely be used as evidence in a court of law.

He rubbed his eyes with the back of his hands like an infant would, tired even in the midst of his panic. He wasn't used to being off-line this long, especially since he'd given up going into work, and although it was definitely illegal to go virtual for more than five hours a day, that was another rule that he had taken to bending quite vigorously. Most people didn't have a choice, government produced programs had a fail-safe cut out. Five hours out of twenty-four was all they would run, no matter how much you swore, and if you decided to have a little tinker around inside and see if you could extend the program yourself, it would log right in to the nearest cop shop. More than one attempt and it was a custodial for you. There was no turning a blind eye for that one.

But the beauty of an illegal program was that there was no cut off point. Sure, they shut down like all the other programs every five hours, to make sure you eat and don't pee in your pants, but then you can start them up twenty minutes later and you're in for another five hours of fun. And that was pretty much how he had lived in recent weeks. Wired up and playing.

He looked longingly at the door to the bedroom where his system was set up. Maybe he should plug in for an hour and try to relax. Maybe then he'd have a life-saving idea. He resisted the urge, but only just. He thought of calling Carol. She was, after all, the only person he knew that could get her hands on that kind of money, but he could just imagine how the conversation would go.

Hi Carol, it's me.

Martin? What are you calling for? You're not due to see the kids until next weekend. Her voice would be cool. *Get out of my life. This is not your allocated day to speak to us. Come back on Saturday, but please don't stay too long.*

Well, the thing is, it's like this. I've got myself in a bit of a financial pickle and need one hundred thousand pounds, preferably in cash. Ideally today or tomorrow. Definitely no later than that. Any chance of a no-way I can repay you loan?

How much did you say? What on earth do you need that kind of money for? What kind of trouble are you in?

Ah. You see, that's the really fun part. When we split up, I heard a really hard time trying to cope, and a crazy part of me thought that I might be able to deal with things better, might be able to concentrate on work, on keeping my head above water, if for a few hours a day I could have my old life back. Sad, huh? So I went to some programmers that weren't strictly legal and they put my old life on disc for me. Sure, that means that unknown to you, they have been in our, sorry, slip of the tongue, your house, watched the kids at play, filmed you naked in the bath, stolen sweat from your tennis gear to get your smell right, rifled through your perfumed underwear, all that kind of great stuff. But, hey, it was all in a good cause. What you didn't know didn't hurt you, did it?

Carol? Are you still there? Are you getting all this?

Anyway, that's all kind of unimportant right now. What is important is that although I did pay a quarter of the cost up front, these things are really rather expensive, and I promised to pay the rest in instalments, which would have been fine if I'd been going in to work, but our life has just been so good in the program that I didn't think that going into work, (I mean real work as opposed to virtual – virtually I've been promoted twice now- are you still with me?), was really that important anymore, and to cut a long story short, it would appear that I've missed a couple of payments, well, four to be exact, and I have a sneaking suspicion they've found out that I've lost my job.

What was that? What will happen if I don't pay up?

Oh well, this is the really great bit. I, me, the me that is, will no doubt have my neck broken in some savage manner, but don't worry about the kids being traumatised, I'll still be along to take them to McDonald's on Saturday, in a manner of speaking of course. In fact, your life won't be affected at all. You probably won't even notice the change. He will be me, after all. And yes, he'll probably beg you to take him back every time he sees you as well.

He started to laugh out loud on the sofa, sitting there in his dressing gown and slippers. If he told her all that there'd be a whole wardrobe full of feet arriving from her Dad in no time at all. His laughter was taking on a manic edge and he found his eyes straying to the bedroom door again. Maybe just half an hour.

He was distracted by a familiar sound that for a moment he just couldn't place, his brown eyes looked quizzically round trying to locate its source, before realising it was the gentle whirr of his front door opening. But that couldn't be. That couldn't be at all. His heart started to speed up, knocking frantically at his ribs, realising the awful truth of the situation well ahead of the rest of him. The only thing that could open his door was a scan of his handprint. *His handprint. His handprint.* No, no, no. Oh, no. God no.

His brain was slowly catching up as the two men walked casually into his living room, one slightly behind the other. The first wore a dark overcoat and was pulling a gun with a silencer attachment from its inner pocket with leather clad hands. He was obviously proud of the traditions of his trade. Despite the fact that the man in front was the one with the gun, *Jesus Christ, he has a gun*, it was the man standing slightly behind him that held Martin's stunned attention.

He was about five feet eleven, with dark hair that couldn't decide whether it was straight or curly, creating the impression that it was tugging his skull in all directions, all except for the fringe which hung lethargically over his dark brown Mediterranean eyes. His hands were pushed far down into his baggy trouser pockets, as he looked awkwardly round the flat, trying desperately not to look at its current owner, obviously wishing he was anywhere but here.

Martin couldn't take his eyes off him, for a moment the danger of the situation forgotten. He was him, and yet not him. The new Martin was slightly heavier, his hair longer. He was also slightly more tanned. In fact the clone looked exactly as he himself had when he had walked into that oversized office, back at the end of summer.

A sharp clicking sound emanating from the man in front brought his attention back to the situation at hand. The gun was armed and pointing confidently in his direction. He drew his eyes away from its dark barrel and into the face of the man holding it. This wasn't right. They had given him two days to get the money. In the corner of his vision he saw his carbon copy slipping away into the kitchen. He almost screamed for him to come back, but pure panic squeezed his throat silent. Something about the way the other him had looked terrified him to the core.

It was the same expression he himself would be wearing if he was about to witness something very bad happening to another human being. Something very nasty and definitely very bloody. The thought of blood made him feel sick. The sight of it made him pass out. It had been the same for the past twenty-four years since he had seen some kid knocked down by a speeder. Knocked down never to get up again. That kid's skull had been flattened and his brain spread generously over the tarmac in clumps, like grey jelly. There was also more blood than he had ever seen, or ever wanted to see again. He could see the look of surprise in those glassy eyes as clearly as he had at six years old. A look that said that a terrible mistake had been made, and that he'd like to change his mind and look both ways now. Martin brought himself back to the present, his vision a tunnel leading into the eternal blackness of the gun barrel that seemed to be oh, so close to the delicate flesh of his face. He could feel his stomach contracting, searching for some hope to cling on to. Please God, he didn't want to be like that kid. Please no, anything but that.

He felt tears springing to his eyes, and could barely keep his trembling lips still enough to force out in a whisper, "But the note said, two days, you said two days, you said…" His voice trailed away as, with the flick of a gloved wrist, the man ushered him onto the sofa.

"Yes, that's right. We did say two days, and two days you would have had if one of the lab boys hadn't got a bee in his bonnet about that mole on your foot."

He didn't understand, didn't understand at all, but at least while they were talking he was still alive. "My foot?" There was more voice than whisper there now, he was pleased to hear, small confidence returning. The stranger wearing the impossibly expensive suit and overcoat, *could you still get real wool these days?*, reached into the open tin box on the table and took a cigarette, sparking it up with a silver Dunhill lighter he pulled from his trouser pocket. He didn't offer Martin one, but started to smoke with a casualness that implied regular use, exhaling a long stream of white chemicals before speaking.

"Yeah, for some reason he seemed to remember that mole. He used to work for the police, so he has a good memory for detail. So anyway, he started checking through the records, and that's when we found out that you weren't Martin 1 at all, but Martin 2." Stubbing out the half-smoked cigarette, he left it alongside Martin's butt from only an hour and a lifetime earlier, and selected a cushion from the sofa, plumping it up.

"Martin 2. What the hell is Martin 2?" Whatever the man was talking about wasn't making any sense, but still managed to make Martin even more uneasy. Uneasy and queasy. His ears had started to ring. The man stopped shaping the cushion and looked him in the eye. Martin didn't like the coldness that sat there so comfortably.

"Do you remember when you and your wife started having problems a couple of years ago?" Martin nodded numbly, no longer sure he wanted to know where this was leading.

"Well, she'd been reading some of the stuff that was going in America and came to the crazy conclusion that maybe by killing you, she might relieve some stress and save your marriage. Burn out all that anger and resentment in one hit. You know what women are like. Especially the rich ones. Too much daytime T.V telling them how unhappy they are all the time." Martin hadn't eaten for over a day, but was still sure that he was going to throw up. This had to be a dream. Either that or he was still in the program and it was corrupting. This could not be real. This could not be happening.

"So anyway, she orders a replacement, and when it's ready, she murders the real Martin in the morning and you gets you activated in the afternoon." The room was spinning now. "As it transpired, and here's the funny part, she couldn't really deal with what she'd done, couldn't shake herself free of the guilt of killing the original you, so rather than having to face it every day, she just kicked you out. I guess she wasn't as American as she originally thought." He laughed aloud as if he had just told a great joke. "Lucky for her she had so much money, or that really would have been a waste of a small fortune."

Whatever it was, one day she just couldn't stand the sight of him anymore.

The man smiled and shrugged. "Ironic really. She should have just saved herself the money and divorced the original you. Anyway, when we called today and told her what trouble her clone had got itself into, she paid your debts instantly. We figured she would, a woman in that position. She even paid for another replacement. Between you and me, I think she's started to think of you as faulty goods. And who can blame her? Living your life on-line is hardly good for your mental health, is it?" He had sat down briefly while speaking, and now rose, still clutching the cushion.

"A new you must seem like the obvious solution to her, wouldn't you say? Especially as she's already done it once. The guilt won't be half as bad second time round." He was nodding to himself as if speaking from experience.

"She just wants a father for her children who's decent. Someone they can look up to. I can understand that, although it's touching coming from the woman that murdered you in the first place, huh?" His voice was light and conversational.

Martin decided that the man was definitely dangerously insane, although that didn't seem that important as the truth of his words started to sink in. The room was had taken on an edge of too much clarity, and he didn't know how much more of this dreamy nightmare he could take. Somewhere in his peripheral vision he saw the man hold out the cushion and come towards him. Carol had killed him. Carol. His Carol. He couldn't get his head round it, and then the cushion was round his head, and the world went black. A fraction of a second later the world went black forever.

Two weeks later and Martin 3 was smiling as he held his daughter's hand on the way back to the car. Sure, seeing Carol had been more painful than he had imagined it would be; the memory of the break up still so fresh for him. The knowledge that she had murdered Martin 1 surprisingly didn't ease that pain, but he knew already that he wouldn't go the path of Martin 2. He had a healthy respect for his ex-wife's ability to replace him at will. Anyway, he had learnt from the mistakes of his predecessor, and he had a much better plan.

He had found, tucked away in the kitchen drawer with his wedding ring, a lock of familiar blonde hair. Written in his hand-writing on the faded paper were two words, "Wedding night." It was weird the little events that got forgotten. Carol lying naked in their hotel bed, looking at him with *so much love*, her eyes bleary from sex, smiling as he cut the single curl from her head, promising to keep it with him forever. She had loved that and she had loved him. God knows why he had kept it after everything went sour. Maybe he just couldn't bring himself to let go of those halcyon times. Anyway, there it had been, waiting patiently for him to come up with the idea.

It might take a while but Martin had started saving hard now that he had got his old job back. He reckoned that within three years, he'd be taking that lock of hair back to his other side of legal friends who just might appreciate the sense of irony. Someone had to save their marriage after all, and there were plenty of accidents a girl could have that could wipe out several years of memory, everything from her wedding night, for example. Tragic, but true. Yes, he thought to himself, as his little girl smiled up at him, her eyes just like her mother's; this could definitely be third time lucky.

THE FEAR

'It's hot in here.'

The writer pulled his tie a little looser, his shirt already sticking to the expanse of belly escaping from his trousers. The sweat stained the red dark silk in patches as if blood was leaking from his pores. God, he needed a drink, a stiff one. How had he got here? And just where *was* here? His head ached trying to remember. It all seemed vaguely familiar, like the hint of a smell long ago forgotten, a sour scent lingering in the stifling air, teasing him with knowledge.

A lazy smile stretched across the tanned Mediterranean face of the man on the other side of the large desk. His manicured fingers drummed out a tango on the worn leather surface as his dark eyes penetrated the writer's flabby cheeks, looking past the network of broken veins spreading like maddened spiders' webs, seeking out his soul. 'You'll get used to it.' The voice was slick; like its owner, smooth and dark. Somewhere outside a gun spat out its load and a woman screamed.

The tiny reflection of the room distorted in the bead of sweat trickling from the balding writer's scalp, a world within a world, its beauty unnoticed. He didn't like this place. It wasn't what he was used to. Not any more.

'Why am I here?' He resented the whine he heard in his words and his leg beginning to twitch beneath him, he scanned the room in search of liquor. Whiskey, rum, gin; shit, even sherry would do. He'd long ago given up pretending to be choosy. When you were worth what he was, you could afford to drink them all. You could afford pretty much anything you wanted when people would pay to read your shopping list if you decided to publish it.

His head swum momentarily and then he found himself seated in the creaking chair behind the tired desk that now bore an old Royale typewriter and a tidy pile of clean, white paper. It was the DTs. Had to be. This whole surreal mess was a hallucination.

The Mediterranean lounged on the desk, cool in linen. 'Why am I here?' He chuckled, repeating the words, tasting them. 'Isn't that the age-old question? So dull and unimaginative. So human. You're all so unsatisfied, aren't you? Always thinking you deserve more. Why can't just *being* be enough?'

Sighing, he stood up, moving like fluid mercury, all ease and sinews, and the writer felt the searing heat of the man's breath on his face.

The man wore snakeskin shoes. They suited him. He gazed out of the small nailed down window, unaware of the scurrying people so far below. A lifetime away. 'You really threw it all out, didn't you? You could have left your mark. You could have touched people, made a difference, but it was all just too much hard work, wasn't it? So, instead you took the easy road and filled the world with more meaningless words for the masses. What a waste. What a failure.'

The writer snorted, jowls wobbling. 'My books make millions worldwide. My readers love me. I'm one of the biggest successes of the twenty-first century. Hardly a failure.'

Still, the words rankled, making a place deep inside him smart and flinch.

A dark eyebrow arched as the man turned back to him. 'Shit sells, baby, shit sells.' His teeth sparkled. 'And you chose shit over substance. That's why you're here. That's why you'll be forgotten in two years.' He snapped his fingers. 'Resigned to the bargain bins.'

The writer's mouth felt too dry for a hallucination. 'What do you want?

'What I want,' he pulled a cigar from his top pocket and lit it, the aromatic smoke absorbing the last of the moisture in the heavy air, 'is a short story.'

The writer laughed, relief flooding through him. A story. A short one at that. He'd be out of here in twenty minutes. He hadn't been quite sure what the man would ask for…but this, this would be easy. He used to write short stories all the time when he was a kid. Before he realized there was no real money in it. He giggled again, and for a moment almost forgot the increasing *need* that was itching at him.

'What did you think I was going to ask for? Your soul?' The amused words drifted towards him from the other side of the room. The man was walking towards the door. With one hand casually tucked into his pocket, he turned and spoke. 'But I don't want shit. I want a story that is true to you. Remember your youth? When your dreams were of Bookers and Pulitzers instead of blondes and Porches? I want a story that will entertain me. I want it to be perfect. I want it to be art.' He paused. 'And when you satisfy my criteria, then you can have that drink you need. In fact, you can have several. Anything you want. As much as you want.'

Watching the man's tapered fingers reaching for the door handle, the writer licked his lips. 'Could I have a small one first? It helps me to write. I...I..I need it.' The words were out, his tone as imploring as his eyes. Just one. That's all he needed. Just one long swallow.

For a brief moment he shut his eyes, almost tasting the fiery liquid, imagining it slipping down his tight throat. When he opened them, his thirst teased alive and unforgiving, the man had gone. More worrying than that, so had the door. The space it had occupied was now just tatty, chipped plaster, blending with the rest of the wall.

The writer's giggle held less humour now, the sound jarring against the emptiness. This craziness was getting weirder and he wondered if he'd finally cracked. One drink too many. One drink too *little* was probably more apt, considering the way his hands were shaking. The keys of the typewriter seemed to blur as he stared at them, but still he took a sheet of the crisp paper and fed it through the roller. A short story. How hard could it be? *I want it to perfect. I want it to be art.* The words echoed in his head. A few plotlines sprung to mind, but he rejected them all. Each one was straight from one of his novels. If he was being honest, then each one belonged to several of his books, reworked slightly and churned out over and over again. Still, how does that saying go?

If it ain't broke don't fix it. That formula had worked just fine for him.

He bit his lip to stop himself prevaricating. This wasn't getting him anywhere. A small slice of life, that's what he needed. A teasing glimpse into another existence. No sub-plot. No back story. Just one small dilemma in need of resolution. But what? His fingers flexed, brushing the old white on black letters. A siren wailed somewhere down in the real world, and for a few minutes he pondered on a crime situation. A dead body discovered. Why and by whom? Maybe the policeman did it? Maybe he's a serial killer on the side? The thin plot was boring him already and he slammed his hand on the desk in frustration.

Okay, he calmed himself, the idea will come. The promise of a drink at the end of this would bring on a plot, of that he was sure. Maybe if he decided on his characters that would help. He let out a long breath. Male or female or a couple of each? No more than four or he'd end up writing a novella. No. No women; including those would turn this into a cliché love story and that wasn't the kind of thing this customer was looking for. He didn't seem like the romantic type. Two men, that's what he needed. Two very different men tied together in a strange situation. Slowly the writer started to smile. The story was coming to him; it was so obvious he couldn't believe he hadn't thought of it before. But how would it turn out? The ending was just a dark hole in front of him, and try as he might he couldn't fill it. Well, the ending could wait. If he was lucky it might just take care of itself.

Still hot as an oven, the room was getting darker and he glanced at his watch. It seemed to have stopped, none of the hands moving, time frozen at 2:20 p.m. How long had he been here? He needed to get started soon or he wouldn't be capable; he'd be far too busy climbing the walls. His hands were poised over the old machine, ready to take care of their work.

So. How to start? Dialogue, that was always an easy way in. Take the audience straight into the action and set up your characters all at the same time. Two birds with one stone. Feeling pleased with himself he started to type, careful not to let his damp fingers slip between the keys.

```
"It's hot in here."
```

As he let the words flow, the world shimmered around him, spinning and twisting until it disappeared into itself, taking him and the typewriter and the words with it.

The devil tapped out a tango on the worn leather desk as he smiled at the writer who twitched for a drink, sweating like a pig just as he had the last time and the time before that and all the countless times previously through the frozen eons of eternity. The devil noticed a small bead of sweat forming on the nervous man's balding head. A world within a world. Perfect. The writer spoke.

'It's hot in here.'

The devil studied the exploding veins on the writer's sallow face. No matter how many times they replayed this little scene, those veins never ceased to fascinate him.

'You'll get used to it.'

Somehow though, he didn't think the writer ever would.

CRYSTAL CARLA

It had been a long day shopping, but as Kevin dumped the carrier bags on the chipped vinyl top of the trailer's breakfast bar, he felt pretty fucking good. He'd got everything he needed, no problemo, even though he'd had to travel pretty far to get the iodine, stuck on the bus next to some greasy fat bitch, her polyester dress itching his skin the whole way. Still it was done now, and the rewards would make it all worthwhile. He tipped out the bag of Sudafed and matches and grinned. Time to get to fucking work. He had habits to feed and cash to collect.

The still, steady heat that burned up the August air outside had turned the confines of the trailer into an oven, and although the place stunk of ripe trash he kept the blinds down and the door shut. Even before he'd needed to keep the prying eyes of the neighbours minding their own goddamn business, he'd kept his trailer shut up during the long summers. Too many damned mosquitoes swarmed in from the swamps out back of the trailer park, hungry for blood, biting you to fucking insanity.

He looked at the pile of ingredients waiting for him to turn them into ice, crystal, glass or whatever fucking else those tweakers wanted to call it. A bug that must've followed him inside buzzed in his ear and he swatted at it angrily. Fucking swamp. Maybe when he'd got more money stashed he'd try and get himself in one of the bigger trailers nearer the front. Away from the flies and the damp and the goddamn white trash.

Ready to get to work, he pulled off his T-shirt ignoring the rank odour of stale sweat that oozed from its pits and his thin body. He'd shower later. Maybe tomorrow before going to his shift at the plant. Who really gave a fuck? You washed and ten minutes later you were dripping like a pig again. No wonder his back was still covered in the zits that had plagued his teenage years and never really left, even though he was pushing thirty in the next couple of years.

Under a cushion on the stained brown sofa his mobile phone burst into life. His personal phone, not his newer, pay-as-you-go business one. Cursing under his breath, he dug around for it and yanked it out. Mike. What the hell did he want on a Sunday afternoon?

'Hey. What's up?' For a few seconds there was only wet, frantic breathing in his ear before Mike finally got his words out.

'Oh, man. Oh man, I gotta see you. Oh shit man...it's Carla...I gotta see you man, you gotta come here now.'

Kevin's skin cooled slightly. What the fuck about Carla? For a second he looked around to where the baseball bat leaned against the door, and then listened again to the hard, shaky air rushing down the phone and reconsidered. Nah, he wasn't going to need the bat. Not yet. Mikey wasn't mad; he was worried. *Scared*.

'What's she done?'

'You gotta come here, Kev. I need you... I need your... help.' Mikey was whining into the phone. What was the crazy bitch up to now?

'I'll be right over.'

Leaving the T-shirt off, he grabbed his keys and let himself back out into the blazing sun, locking the door. Not that he really needed to. No one was going to rob him, and if they tried he'd hear the dog before they'd got anywhere near the door. Still it was always better to be safe than sorry and kids could be stupid. Walking past the heavy Rottweiller that was tucked panting under the shade of the plastic barbecue table, he bent to pat him on the head.

'Kill any fucker that tries to fuck us up, Cujo.'

The dog let out a small gruff bark before resuming his heavy, hot breathing, head resting between his paws. The lazy look was a good disguise. There was no-one in the park that wanted to mess with Cujo; he had a mean streak of madness in his eyes sometimes, that was for sure, and Kevin made sure he treated the dog with nothing but respect. Anything that could rip your throat out on a whim deserved that.

Mike and Carla's trailer was two rows behind his, the last line before the swamps, and the midges and flies filled the air along with the stink of the stagnant water. Every time he came back here, Kev's own row didn't seem so bad. People that lived in the last row were the trailer trash of the trailer trash people, and that was something no one wanted to be, even in a society outcast from the rest.

He banged on the closed door.

'It's me, Mikey. Open up.'

Funny how things changed. Until the problems with Carla, Mike had lived right up the other end of the park, near all the facilities and where the front of the homes had little gardens fenced off and the residents made sure they whitewashed their trailers at least once every couple of years and kept their rows free of litter. Shit, if it wasn't for Carla, Mike would probably have moved out of the park completely by now.

Kev had only come to know Mike from working for a while on the same section of the plant. That's how he'd first met Carla. She'd brought Mike in his lunch every day, back then. Thick cut sandwiches and a flask of fresh coffee, her hair pulled back in a ribbon, pretty pink lipstick matching the flowers in her home-made summer dresses. All the men would stop and watch when Carla brought Mike his lunch in a kind of awe. Where the hell did a man find a wife like that? That's what they were thinking, Kevin included. And all the men would watch when Carla waved and walked away, because as well as being an angel, Carla was one fine sweet piece of ass.

The door opened an inch, Mike's eyes peering fearfully round the edge before his arm came out and pulled Kev into the gloom. He shut the door behind them and paced in a little circle, his hands rising up to his head and then back down again in frantic little movements.

'She just wouldn't shut up, Kevin, she just wouldn't shut up and she just kept cussing me and telling me to get her what she needed and I was telling her she needed to break this, she'd done two days she could do some more, but she wouldn't shut up and she didn't even look like Carla any more...'

'What the fuck are you talking about, Mikey? Get to it.'

Mike stared at him, his face pale under untidy dark hair. His tongue flicked out over his lips and for a moment he looked like he was going to cry. 'I think I killed her, Kev. I think I killed my Carla.'

Kevin felt that slight chill on his skin again. *Carla dead?* His brain felt sludgy.

'Where is she?'

Letting out a whimper, Mike stopped circling and stared over at the plastic sheeting that hung down separating the kitchen area.

'Her fucking teeth had started to fall out, Kev. I mean, Jesus, she just needed to stop with all that shit but she just wouldn't try and then she just wouldn't shut up…'

Pushing past him Kevin lifted the sheet and stepped in. There was sawdust and various cupboard doors spread around. He almost smiled. Mikey didn't belong down this end of the park. He *cared* too much. Who the fuck put a new kitchen in the shit-holes down here? People like Mikey, that's who. One new door hung away from the wall unfinished, and looking down Kevin could see why. The required screwdriver was sticking out of Carla's neck.

'Holy shit, Mikey.' It was hard to keep the disgust out of his voice. Carla alive had been looking pretty fucking rotten recently, but Carla dead was worse. The skin that had prematurely wrinkled and aged now hung slack from her face, postules on her cheeks still leaking slightly from where she'd probably been picking at them in her junkie anxiety, and her wide yellowing eyes stared dully at the ceiling as if she couldn't even manage surprise at her own violent death.

'You say she was trying to go straight?'

Mike's breath hitched a little, wet and slick. 'No…not really. I was trying to get her to stop… I was trying… I was trying to get her back, my Carla back…not this thing… and I thought if I made her stop long enough…' Mike's voice drifted off as the slow weight of what he'd done settled on him. After a pause, he was stronger. 'I wanted her to tell me what fucker had got her into this. I wanted to know who gave it to her.'

Kev felt goosebumps rise a little on his slick skin. 'And?'

'She wouldn't say. Now I'll never fucking know.'

His heart thumping too hard with relief, Kevin looked down at Carla, and bit his cheeks to stop from laughing right out loud. Carla gone. Really gone. Thank fuck for good old Mikey 'cause Kev knew, he'd known for sometime, that Carla was going to spill one day soon, and then Mike was going to come for him. That was why he'd started keeping the baseball bat close to the door. Just in case.

'What are we going to do with her?'

Mike looked up. 'I figure I'd better call the cops. Hand myself in.'

'Are you crazy? That bitch fucked up your life enough already. You can't do time for her as well.' He paused. 'You would never survive a long stretch, man. You know that.'

'But…'

'No fucking buts.' He stared at Mike long and hard. 'We both know you didn't call me just so's you could call the cops.' He grabbed the electric saw from the newly fitted worktop. 'This is what we'll do. Cut her up and then fucking throw her into the swamp. All in bits like that the alligators will have her eaten up in no time. Gone like she was never here.'

'But Jesus man, that's Carla. My Carla.'

'No it isn't. Look at her. She hasn't been your Carla in a long time.' His nose crinkled a little. 'You probably put her out of her misery, man. She was never going to break that habit. She was in too deep. Everyone could see that.'

Sweat was breaking through the thin fibre of Mike's vest top. 'But won't people notice that she's gone? Won't people…'

'No one gives a shit what happens to people down here, Mike. You know that. I'll just put it around that you've kicked her out. No one will ask questions. Trust me.'

Mike nodded. 'Okay.' He swallowed hard. 'Let's do it.'

'You got any more of that plastic shit?'

Mike nodded, his face pale.

'Then maybe you should try and cover up as much of your kitchen as you can. And I think we should strip.'

After five long minutes prepping themselves, they locked eyes and Kevin fired up the saw. 'You hold her. I'll cut.' There was no way that Mike was going to be able to do the dirty end; he'd puked his fucking guts up once already and they hadn't even started. Jesus. 'But hold her good. Let's get this done fast. Then as soon as the sun's down we can dump her. We'll take some of those old cupboards out too. Anyone watching will think we're just ditching trash.'

Kev figured that Mike held it together pretty good all things considered. Cutting down from her left shoulder and between the dried out tea bags that had once been the most lusted over pair of titties this side of the Keys, Kev gripped the saw that juddered through the bone, and by the time the top of her torso fell heavily away, both men were covered by the dark, sticky spray. The heat in the kitchen was getting stifling and even Carla's dead blood stunk rotten against their naked skin. Mikey gagged but held it down. Kev was pretty impressed. He was fighting the feeling himself and he was fucking glad the bitch was dead.

'You okay, man?'

Mike let out a small hysterical giggle. 'No, I'm not shitting okay, but don't for fuck's sake stop.'

Looking down at the wreck of the body, Kev knew his own limitations. If he cut through her gut then they'd have to deal with all those slick fucking entrails coming out and he'd seen enough movies to know he didn't want anything to do with that. No way did he want to be picking up her guts and stuffing them back inside her. He'd cut her legs off and be done with it. Four pieces was enough. The alligators could do the rest of the fucking job.

It was all over in ten minutes and his hands still red and wet, Kev pulled two beers from the dirty refrigerator, cracking them open on the side. Mike downed his then staggered to the john covering his mouth. By the time he came back out ten minutes later, Kev had got Carla's quarters tied up in trash bags.

They downed a second beer each before Kevin spoke. 'Guess we'd better clean up. You on nights tonight?' His voice sounded surprising normal. But then he felt pretty good, all things considered. Carla was gone. Dead and gone. And he hadn't had to do a thing.

'Yeah man, but I can't fucking work, not after this... can't I just come back to yours and ...'

Kev thought of the ingredients sitting in his own trailer and the customers he had waiting, *needing* him to get his job done. 'No. you gotta work, man. You gotta pretend this fucked-up shit didn't happen. Pretend you just kicked her out.' He finished his beer. 'Pretend long enough and you'll believe it.' He looked around him. 'Now let's get this shit cleaned up. Then we need to shower, dress and dump all this crap in the swamp.'

By ten he was back in his own trailer, crushing up the Sudafed tablets, his shoulders aching slightly from clearing out Mike's kitchen and Carla's remains. Mike had gone to the plant, and although he was shaken, Kevin could see that he wouldn't talk. His eyes were too clear for that. For now at any rate, they were safe.

Scraping the pile of powder from the chopping board and into the bowl of alcohol, Kevin whistled. He was feeling pretty fucking good. The problem of Carla had been resolved and he was in the clear. Hally-fucking-luyah. And he'd learnt his lesson. Don't shit in your own backyard. Not with someone like Mikey. He didn't need people from the plant knowing about his other income, and as he would never be so fucking stupid to take the shit himself, no one even suspected that he dealt in crystal. And that's the way it would stay.

Yeah, getting Carla hooked had been pretty stupid but seeing her everyday, her ripe body outlined through the cotton of her clothes, had driven him crazy and how the fuck else was he ever going to be able to fuck her? He hadn't even planned it. He'd been finishing his shift and she was walking back from bringing Mike his lunch and they'd walked together. Fuck, he could remember how hard it was to keep his eyes on her eyes and not those fucking peachy tits as they'd talked. He couldn't remember the shit she was saying, something about starting a fucking family, but he *could* remember her tits and the way his dick had been getting too hard in his pants.

He'd invited her in for lemonade, and she hadn't been sure, he could see that in her awkwardness, but she was too polite to say no. They ended up having a beer and it went straight to her pretty little head, and then they were talking about their teenage years and he was making her laugh and relax, and she said how she'd smoked some weed when she was in school and she'd never laughed so much since.

And then it came to him. Just like that. He told her he had a little rock of cannabis saved for a special occasion and why the hell didn't they just smoke it and laugh this hot afternoon away, and although he expected her to say no, she'd said yes, what the hell, a little weed never did no-one no harm, did it?

He'd loaded two pipes. His with the hash, hers with the ice. He lit his first, letting the strong sweet smell reassure her, and then he lit hers. And oh boy, did she rush. She took to the ice like she was born to it, and it took to her right back. Within minutes she was touching herself and him, and all afternoon he fucked her every which way he could and she loved every fucking depraved second of it. Women on ice will fuck like whores every time and Carla was no exception. He'd done things to her he'd only ever dreamed about a woman letting him do, and by the time she came down they were both bruised and exhausted.

She cried then; oh fuck did she cry, before scurrying off to scrub herself clean before her beloved Mike came home, but by then Kev didn't really give a shit. Who the fuck took drugs from a virtual stranger? Especially a woman that looked like that? A stupid cunt, that's what she was, and when he'd shut the door behind her, he never expected to hear from her again. But the ice or her shame had got its hold on her and within two days she was back, not able to look him in the eye, but the trembling in her hands told him everything he needed to know.

Yep, he thought, carefully filtering the liquid, those first couple of months of feeding Carla's habit and banging her ice-horny ass all afternoon, had been fun, but then the crystal got hold of her *outside* too and then she stopped looking so good.

He'd still given her the dope for free; he didn't want her running her rotten mouth to Mike, but he didn't want to fuck her anymore. Sometimes he'd let her give him head, but desperation was never a turn on and if he wanted to fuck a junkie then there were better looking ones that he could choose from. One of the perks of the job.

But now Carla was gone, and business could get back to normal, no harm done. A weight had lifted from him, and Mike had been the one to take care of it. Life was fucking funny sometimes, the way it turned around.

He looked at his watch. Half-ten. He'd be lucky if he had any shit to sell by tomorrow at this rate.

At two a.m., one batch of ice was finally ready for the next day's *needers* and Kev was just about to go to bed when Cujo barked outside. Nothing major, just a couple of low gruff warning growls. Irritated more than worried, Kevin stepped out into the humid night. Cujo was at the end of the trailer staring out towards the swamp, his whole body alert.

'Cujo? What's up man?'

The dog didn't respond to the low call of his name, but at least stopped growling. After a couple of seconds he whimpered and then sat, his head cocked slightly. Kevin watched him carefully for a minute before shrugging and going back inside. Whatever the fuck was bothering the dog it obviously wasn't that big a deal. Maybe the alligators were moving around in the swamp. The thought made him smile. *Goodnight, Carla. Sweet fucking dreams.*

He stripped down to his pants and lay on the untidy bed in the dark. Fuck, he was tired. It had been a long fucking day. Beside him, his phone beeped, and checking it he saw it was a message from Mike. Saying thank you for what he'd done. Tossing the phone to the floor, he shut his eyes, letting his mind drift to sleep, a small smile on his face. Yeah, it was a funny fucking world where Mike was grateful to him for helping deal with Carla.

The banging on his trailer door woke him with a start, sweat itching at his skin. Fuck it was hot. And who the fuck was that, waking him up in the middle of the night? They wouldn't fucking do it again, he thought pulling on his trousers. That was for fucking sure.

Flicking on the light in the main living area, he was glad he'd tidied all the shit away before going to bed. It was probably Mike outside, just finished his shift and wanting to talk. Always wanting to fucking talk, that was Mikey. It was more than time to cut that friendship loose, especially after today. The door banged again.

'Hang the fuck on,' he muttered, undoing the bolt and yanking the door open, a swarm of swamp mosquitoes flooding into the light.

He stared. It seemed he stared for a long time before the

thing on the doorstep spoke, breaking the illusion that this must be some shitting fucking dream.

'*I need… I need a fix, baby. I need you to fix me up….*'

His own breath locked in his lungs, Kevin stepped backwards, revolted, and Carla followed him inside. She'd pulled herself back together as best she could, but as she moved the wet, sawn edges of her jigsaw puzzle body slipped and slid against each other, showing flashes of her red, dead meat.

'This isn't real. This isn't fucking real.' Kev spoke the words out loud trying to hold his brain in one piece at least as well as Carla was holding her body together.

His back bumped into the breakfast bar, halting his progress, and she manoeuvred herself awkwardly forward, one hesitant step at a time until she was right in front of him.

Kev felt his stomach flip and turn and drop in the same second. Oh fuck she looked so real, her yellow eyes staring right into his, and a small yelp escaped him. She stank of the swamp and in the division between her breasts where he'd sawed them apart earlier that day he could see some small fronds of plant life poking through.

'*I need some ice, baby, I need you to ice me up like you always did, baby. I need it so bad…and Mikey wouldn't let me…*'

Her tongue was still pink as it poked out, the words almost guttural, her breath stagnant like the water she'd dragged herself from, but the desperate whine in her voice was all Carla. All junkie Carla.

Resisting the urge to giggle or throw up, Kevin took a deep breath. Maybe this was just a fucking dream. It was natural he'd dream of Carla and the ice tonight. Maybe he should just see the dream through. Yeah. That was it. Or maybe he'd just tripped out on all the chemicals. No need to freak. No need to LOSE HIS FUCKING MIND. Just keep his head down and give the fucking nightmare what it wanted.

Slipping past her, not wanting to touch, he kept his vision forward and opened the fridge. His sweating hand shook way too much as he pulled the box out. He hated the solidity of it in his fingers. It was too real, too fucking real. *Did things in dreams, even tripped out ones, feel this real? Don't think like that now. Just a dream, man. Just a fucking dream.* Putting it on the breakfast bar, he reached into one of the cupboards for a pipe, trying to ignore the happy damp sigh from the Carla thing as she saw the drugs.

Trying not to look at her, *but fuck it's hard not, and look how fucking hungry for this shit her dead eyes are*, he stuffed the pipe with rocks and handed it over. The arm that was still attached to her head and neck grabbed at it, locking it into her dead mouth, the other reaching for the box of matches. Her damp fingers soaked the box, the match only fizzing slightly, and not able to watch her angry frustration, Kevin grabbed another box from beside the stove. His own hands were shaking so badly that he almost dropped the match as he lit it. *Some fucking crazy shit dream. Maybe he should wear gloves when mixing the chemicals from now on, oh yeah, maybe that's what he should do.*

When the pipe was lit, he stepped back, his gaze drawn onto Carla, despite himself. Her eyes shut as she blissfully drew the heavy smoke in, Kevin watching in horror as it leaked out through all the gaps between her reassembled body parts. When she finally opened her eyes again, he was crying. There was only so much of shit like this he could take.

'Why don't you just go now, Carla?' He pushed the box across the breakfast bar. 'Take it all with you if you want.' There was a whine in his own voice and he didn't like it. He didn't like it one bit. Why wouldn't she just fucking disappear like bad dreams were supposed to?

Carla leaned over the breakfast bar and Kevin moaned, knowing that her legs would be standing upright, bloody stumps visible, as her body tilted away from them. Her tongue darted out between her lips.

'Oh but baby, now I need something else...You know what I need...'

He stared at her confused for a moment, before with dread he took in her posture; torso forwards, ruined breasts squeezed together between her arms, and then realised what she was doing. It was a disgusting parody of flirtation.

'Oh no.' Bile rose steaming into his chest. 'Oh no fucking way, you dead bitch..' He stumbled backwards towards the bedroom as she found her legs again and came round the breakfast bar towards him. 'No fucking way...'

'But I'm so horny, Kevin, you know the ice makes me horny and you always used to want to fuck me so bad...' She grinned, and something

from the swamp wriggled out from under her tongue. '*And now you can fuck me all night Kevin…. And I can fuck you and we don't have to worry about Mikey any more…*'

And then she was touching him, swamp breath on his skin, and squeezing his eyes shut, Kevin hid somewhere deep inside with what was left of his sanity.

The next morning, he woke with a start, rolling out of his bed and onto the floor, stomach heaving before his eyes were even open. Flashing revolting images filled his head. *Carla's dismembered body riding him. Carla forcing his head down…* He shook the mental picture away. Fuck man, that dream was something else. Too much fucking something else. Shivering and fighting waves of nausea, he sat on the floor for a few minutes before trusting his legs to stand. Outside the sun shone brightly and he took strength from it. Fucking Carla was dead. That was the truth, and however real that nightmare had seemed, it was only a dream. Nothing more.

Going into the kitchenette, he paused when he saw the ice box still on the side, not in the refrigerator. Okay. So maybe he'd been sleepwalking. No big deal. In fact, that helped some things make sense. It would explain maybe why the dream had been so vivid. His heart pumped with relief. Yeah, that *did* make sense. Thank fuck for that.

Putting the drugs and pipe back, he grabbed a tin of food and went out to feed Cujo, but the dog was gone. Kev called him, but there was no answer. After five minutes he came back inside, shut out the heat and threw the can into the bin. Fucking dog. He should have kept him on a chain. He'd been meaning to but never got round to it. Still, he'd be back when he'd finished chasing some bitch no doubt, and then he could go fucking hungry. For a little while at least. His bare foot squashed something slimy and he lifted it.

A swamp slug. He stared at it. His stomach chilled. He remembered it wriggling out from under her tongue. Right in that spot.

The day never really settled down after that.

When Carla came the second night, her tongue was turning

black and she stank worse than before, her flesh sweating and stinking, stomach swollen with gases. His mind cracking as he watched her shuffle into the trailer, Kevin figured that death and decomposition hadn't really slowed her down much. Hadn't slowed her habit down either. He'd never really thought about how much ice could really get you before, but now he was. Oh now, he was thinking about it a whole big deal.

She had Cujo with her, one of the dog's hind legs missing where maybe a swamp alligator had bitten it off either before or after he was dead. That didn't seem to slow him down much neither. His growl was still vicious and Kev reckoned his bite would be too.

While he was getting her fix together, Carla told Kevin in no uncertain terms what Cujo would do to him if he tried to leave her. Not that it would count for much, because she'd always find him. She needed him too much. And wasn't that what he'd wanted? For her to need him? And now he had her. Forever.

He watched her taking in the ice, and then watched as she came towards him, displaced hips wiggling, cracked mouth oozing dirty words that not so many months ago he'd fantasized too much about hearing her speak, and now made his soul tremble. Watching her coming, seeing his future ahead of him, he finally knew that there were many kinds of nightmares and sometimes they were real even if they still only came at night.

Laughing and crying, he reached for the pipe and stuffed it with crystal, managing one long inhale, hoping it might just make it bearable, before he felt her clammy hands on his trousers.

THE HOSTS

The first time Clare saw one of the creatures for herself was on the flight home from Hong Kong, when a thin length of segmented tail (or head?) extended from the ear of another couple's adopted baby. That explained why the poor little girl had been crying so much; and here Clare had just thought the changes in air pressure might be hurting her ears.

There had been four couples going together as a group – three straight couples and a pair of lesbians – to bring home their babies at last. Clare had known that the babies would fuss with discomfort, and this would make the other passengers uncomfortable as well, but they would all just have to endure it together. And so she had reclined her seat against the knees of the man behind her, trying to make a cushy bed of her body for the boy they had named Dylan. Despite all her zealous dieting programs, she had a large body presumably made for birthing children, though she had not been successful in that endeavor, either. Her husband, Gary, had an even larger body, imposingly tall and broad but more successfully toned from racquetball and bike riding. He took turns cradling their tiny new son, so unlike them with his dark hair standing up in wispy spikes and his glistening black eyes. The four babies looked more like siblings than they did relations to their new mothers, who were uniformly blond – though in Clare's case, anyway, not in the natural sense. But Dylan's differences didn't cause his new parents concern. Rather, it would announce to others the generousness of their hearts, in that they had obviously gone so far in their efforts to give a child from a less privileged country the opportunity for a better life. They expected most people to be charmed and admiring, rather than confounded. Celebrities did this all the time.

"My favorite souvenir," Gary joked, kissing his squirming son on the top of his head. Whenever he moved his big body, he accidentally dropped a burping towel or teething ring or cover to a baby bottle behind him, so that the passenger crushed back there would have to dig down at his feet to retrieve it. Oh well. He'd just have to understand how important this all was.

The couple ahead, at least, understood. With a little girl of their own, they had been excitedly babbling to Clare and Gary over their seat like neighbors over a fence between neatly groomed yards. It was during one of these moments, when the other couple were holding their baby up to see Dylan, distracting their infant long enough for her bawling to subside into mere sniffles, that the animal inside her skull snaked about six inches of its body out of her ear to test the air lazily, before sliding moistly back inside.

Clare had been shocked silent. The father holding his new child up like a hard-won trophy had cried out in horror and held her up higher, as if to throw her away from himself in an impulsive act of revulsion, as if a porcelain doll had broken open in his hands to reveal itself filled with excrement. Only after he and his wife began blurting loudly and miserably, and Gary said, "*What? What?*" did Clare begin to tremble hard and mumble over and over, "Oh my God."

And then she remembered that her own adopted child had been crying a lot during the long, long flight, too.

✶　✶　✶

"Hi, honey; do you need a ride to the –"

That was all that Clare's friend Patricia got out before her fourteen-year-old daughter Brice slapped her across the face with cracking force, and strode off to her room upstairs. They heard her door slam, and urban music come thumping to life like the dramatic beat of her teenage heart.

"I'm sorry," Patricia said to Clare, turning to her with a mix of stunned pain and embarrassment. She smoothed her hair back over her reddened ear. "She's going through a tough time right now. I guess her boyfriend has stopped talking to her, and kids tease her sometimes about Chad – you know."

Clare knew, despite having no other children. According to

the experts on talk shows and in counseling classes, older siblings of those carrying the parasite often exhibited resentment arising from feelings that, in attending to their more physically afflicted younger brothers or sisters, their parents weren't giving them sufficient attention. Thus, there were really two kinds of affliction sweeping the country's children.

Like most flu strains, apparently, the parasite was thought to have originated in Asia. Of course Clare had heard of it before witnessing a case for herself on the plane; it had been hard to miss on the news. But it had all seemed so far away, as removed from her world as conditions like elephantiasis, brought about by nematodes and other parasites, better known but still inconceivable to Clare in this day and age. In her subsequent research (and she prided herself on how much research she had done, comparing notes with her friends in support class), Clare had read about other parasites that had harassed human beings through the millennia. Tapeworms thirty feet in length, sometimes expelled from the mouth. Round-worms and their like vomited up, or inching their way out through the penis, or burrowing out the navel. Lumbricoid worms inside the ears, the nose. Worms inside the human heart.

It all seemed so – Third World. So Dark Ages. And yet here they were, almost seven years later, and the parasite that afflicted Dylan had spread around the globe like a communicable virus. Seven years later, and it was all just a sad fact of life in even the most privileged of countries.

"You handle it well," Clare said to Patricia. It was the kind of thing they all said to each other, all the time, in and out of the classes. "I know it's hard with a teenager, even without a host-kid." It was what they called them.

"Well, how about you? Sometimes I don't know how you do it alone, Clare."

"Oh, Gary sees Dylan every other weekend, and usually at least one evening during the week. He's still a good father, I have to give him that." Clare had straightened up her body in her chair in order to pay her ex-husband these compliments. She had to show her grace, her strength, even as it ate at her that after almost ten years of marriage her husband had left her for another woman. Blonder, much more slender. And now, pregnant. She hoped it wouldn't be a host-kid, she really did. After all, what kind of self-respecting, mature, well-balanced adult would hope otherwise?

"Here's our little guys now," Patricia said, smiling fondly, as her son Chad and Dylan came into her livingroom.

They came like two frat boys who'd been drinking too hard, stumbling and bumping into each other and half leaning on each other. Chad was crying. He looked beat up and feverish and ill-rested all at once. Mucus glistened thickly over his upper lip, and he licked at it. Patricia sped over to him to wipe it away. "Don't lap it, honey, how many times have I told you?" She also dabbed away a trickle of the stuff that had run down his neck out of his ear. She rubbed vigorously at the collar of his expensive sweater. Next she dabbed his eyes; the wetness leaking from them might not consist solely of tears.

Dylan wasn't crying, but he looked drugged, his gaze meandering around the room as if he couldn't distinguish his mother from the furnishings. Actually he *was* drugged, for pain and to keep the parasites' growth, activity and reproduction in check, though there was no way yet that could be found to poison the parasites entirely or root them out fully without involving delicate brain surgery. Clare went to him and took his hand and his befuddled eyes found her at last. It seemed like the last time they had looked bright and alive had been on that flight home from Hong Kong, so many miles and years before.

Well, she still prized those dark slanted eyes. But though she had studied Chinese culture extensively, and admired it to the degree that she felt would be expected of her, she couldn't help but congratulate herself that here she was taking such very good care of a little boy from a country where murdering healthy infants simply for being female had once been so widespread. It was her responsibility, as an educated and sophisticated human being, to represent her species in a much more civilized and enlightened fashion. It was all about courage, tenacity, personal grit. Patience, balance, and endurance. Endurance above all else. These qualities had served her well in college, and in the workplace. She had never known they would also become such valuable resources in this way.

These qualities were what enabled her to smile into her son's face, as he looked up at her now, even with the bulge protruding from his brow where some of his parasites – a dozen in number, the most recent scans indicated – had bored through his skull and laid a cache of eggs under the flesh. The doctors reassured her that they felt these eggs wouldn't hatch, since being so close to the surface like this had made it easier and safer to inject enough of a solution to prevent the larvae from developing. Hopefully. But Dylan still bore scars on other parts of his head (patches of hair were missing or growing back unevenly) where clusters of newborn worms had spontaneously erupted. They couldn't all be sustained within the narrow confines of a single brain, so it was their habit to lay their eggs and hatch nearer to the surface, in order to spread afield in search of other hosts. (And it was still being determined why they only chose children from newborns to adolescence.) It was just the occasional stray worm that lost its way back inside the head, and got too comfortable to seek egress again, that caused their numbers to grow within a single host. Not that there hadn't been exceptions. Hosts who eventually died, their brains found to house colonies of a hundred worms or more.

The bulge on Dylan's forehead could be seen pulsing, if you looked closely and in a certain light. Throbbing like a second, ailing brain feeding off his own. And it was only when Dylan sniffed that Clare spotted the tip of a parasite, maybe a blind head taunting her, before it disappeared back inside the boy's nostril.

Meeting her eyes, Dylan said, "The host-boy kicked us. Chad worm-child kicked our extremity. Shit shit fucker."

"Now, honey," she told the seven-year-old, not wanting to upset her friend by showing any resentment toward her child; you had to be as understanding of them as you were your own. "I'm sure Chad didn't mean it."

"We want to break kill eat peanut butter on toast mom-worm. *Now!*" He kicked her sharply in the shin. Always the shin. The host-kid moms joked in class that their black-and-blue shins were their badge of honor.

Clare winced and said, "Okay, honey, I'll take you home now

and make you some toast with peanut butter."

"Tuna sandwich! Tuna sandwich, sow-mom!" He bubbled his lips at her, speckling her face with saliva and parasite mucus, and then he squeezed her hand warmly and started leading her toward the door.

"Catch you later, Pat!" Clare called over her shoulder. "The prince is whisking me off!"

"I can see that," Patricia said brightly, although she was struggling with her own son to keep his hands off her breasts. "See you in class."

They both heard the door to Brice's bedroom door slap open upstairs, the violent music boom louder, and the teenager shriek down at them, "Keep the noise down, you stupid fucks – I'm on the phone to Brad!"

* * *

The parking lot of Dylan's school gleamed with ranks of SUVs, like an army of giant beetles in readiness for world domination. They were owned by parents come to see their children play soccer in the field behind the school. The parents perched on opposing bleachers, trying to look composed and good-natured but each inwardly praying that the coaches – especially trained to work with host-kids – could keep their children in line, like diligent dogs herding an unruly flock. Soccer had been a great way for a lot of these kids to focus their attention and channel their aggression. (Their disgruntled older siblings contented themselves with sports on video game consoles, though they tended to prefer games involving shooting sprees.) Of course, it had sometimes proved disastrous to mix host-kids and "typical" kids on the same teams, or have host-kids teams oppose "typicals," and so the schools now kept these teams and events separate.

But not all host-kids responded well; a lot of it had to do with how many parasites the individual child contained, and how they affected his or her particular brain. Clare had hoped that she could sit proudly in her class and report on her child's successes, as did Melissa and Dawn and other moms whose kids had reaped therapeutic benefits from the sport, chasing and kicking the ball as if to kick the very worms out of their own skulls. Dylan, though, just wasn't into the whole thing, as was evidenced by the kick he had just delivered to his mom's shin instead of a soccer ball.

He panted red-faced and sweaty-haired by the side of the field, Clare hovering over him as Coach Chandler left them alone together to go address some other dilemma. Dylan had had to be taken out of the game for flopping down on his back in the middle of the field and shouting obscenities, much to Clare's chagrin, though she tried to countenance that display and the pain in her leg with calm and composure.

"Honey, this is supposed to be fun," she told him.

"No fun no fun chase sterile egg we don't like soccer."

"Well *we* don't like your attitude, young man. You've got to have more patience."

The boy snapped his eyes to hers, suddenly looking less distracted than he had before. "Who is *we*? Are you our queen?"

"Now honey," she sighed with irritation in her tone, reserved for times when no one else could hear and think she might be losing control, "you know I'm your mom. I told you, don't let those pests talk for you. You have to work on that."

"You call us prince your prince so you are our queen!" he whined, growing more agitated. Clare flinched, expecting another kick, but his shoe scuffed at the asphalt instead.

"Okay, okay, I'm your queen." She took his hand and began walking him away toward the parking lot briskly, looking over to give a little shrug to Coach Chandler as if it didn't ruffle her much, though it secretly irked her that other kids continued to run and play behind her, their parents no doubt glowing with pride – when not twisting their hands in their laps with dread that their child's meltdown would come next. "Let's just get home now so I can start thinking about dinner."

"We want queen take us to king Burger King!"

"Whatever," she sighed.

By the time they reached the rows of vehicles, however, her embarrassment was easing up already. Dragging him to their SUV had been like carrying a splintered cross upon her shoulders, while keeping her back as straight as possible, no sweat marring her expensively casual sweatshirt and jeans. Her poise counterbalanced her son's chaos. Parents watching her retreat would feel less sorry for her than praiseful of her personal dignity. She epitomized the order that their children – their society – needed to get through all this.

*   *   *

At last, Clare thought she had found something Dylan could take part in that would improve his social interaction, or at least upon which he could concentrate some of his turbulent energy. She was encouraged by the new class she was trying out on Wednesday nights, over in the city of Worcester. The class was called the Hive Moms, and the program they sponsored was called the Hive Chorus. The group's approach was to confront and direct their children's malady by "fighting hive mind with hive mind."

"These worms aren't going to claim our kids," Hive Moms' founder, Paula, would say, her own twin girls having been infested. "It's time to take our kids back and show these things who's really in charge."

It seemed that many host-kids liked to sing, and could sustain their attention throughout not only the course of a song, but a whole concert of songs. Apparently the parasites liked it, found it soothing when a group of children invaded with them bonded to a united purpose in such a way. It was a kind of harmony, as soothing to the moms as to the parasites they were in competition against.

A reporter from a Boston-based newspaper was in attendance at tonight's concert in the auditorium of Dylan's school, an event Clare had helped Paula organize. Clare heard the reporter ask Paula, "But might this kind of program be as beneficial to the parasites as it is to the kids? Obviously they're getting something out of it themselves, since the host-kids take to singing so much."

"Well," Paula replied, unfazed, "even if that's the case, that still works for us, because while we are determined that our kids' identities won't be eclipsed, and determined to evict these pests someday, in the meantime we have to deal with what we've got, and it's undeniable that the worms are integrated in their minds. So if that's the situation, and we can't oust the worms at this point, then we at least have to help our kids live with them. And that means not only directing our children's minds constructively, but directing the worms' minds constructively along with them."

Clare smiled. She couldn't have said it better.

That night the children didn't speak in tongues, but sang in the voices of angels. Clare clasped her hands together in pride as she watched them, and swept her gaze across the delighted (and relieved) faces of the audience. For the closing songs – Bette Midler's "Wind Beneath My Wings" and Whitney Houston's "Greatest Love of All" – the whole group of kids sang together, the stage filled with their little bodies and the air above their heads golden with their music. So many host-kids, and yet this was only one room in one town in this whole big country. For a moment, seeing the mass of their bodies clustered like one huge organism, Clare had a shuddering moment when she reflected that this was essentially a generation, and was thus the possible future of humanity. But she quickly brightened. With the help of devoted parents like herself, at least this generation would possess some kind of structure and order.

The applause was thunderous. Clare had tears in her eyes. Proud of Dylan. Proud of herself. She felt a sense of vindication.

Even her ex-husband Gary, his new wife with her cutely rounded belly beside him as if they rode together in cramped airplane seats, looked over at Clare and smiled, nodded. She felt even more vindicated, and smiled back, trying not to feel smug. (So unbecoming.)

Thank God she had found the Hive Moms! They were definitely the best group she had tried yet. There was even one mom, Leslie, who had introduced Clare to a cosmetic surgeon who promised to minimize some of the scarring on Dylan's head. Leslie had used the surgeon to reduce the Down's Syndrome look of her own son. A son with Down's Syndrome and a daughter with the parasite! Leslie was an inspiration; all the Hive Moms were. Their motto had become a chant, their chant the droning buzz of their own determined hive mind. And that motto was: if you can not conquer, endure.

After the concert, Gary and his pet wife met Clare and Dylan in the parking lot to congratulate them. Gary hugged his son, and absent-mindedly brushed at the smear of mucus on his jacket afterwards. "Great job, champ, great job!"

"We thank you," Dylan said to him. He then reached out to touch his stepmom's belly but she jerked back a little.

Bitch, Clare thought, indulging herself tonight with one sugary spoonful of undignified nastiness.

The cars began pulling away, dispersing toward their respective homes. Clare was one of the last to go, after having stayed to say goodnight to most of the other parents, basking in her satisfaction at having helped set up tonight's show. Dylan was fairly patient throughout this but at last she had to buckle his squirming body into the seat beside her and drive off in her own SUV.

"I was so, so proud of you tonight, honey. Thank you so much."

"It is for you."

"Huh?" She looked over at him as she drove. "No, honey, it's for you. This is all to help you, not me."

In the vehicle's murky interior, his narrow black eyes glittered a bit disconcertingly. For that moment he appeared not only to be of a different race, but of a different species; something from another world or branch of evolution. His bristly black hair stirred, and she realized one of the parasites had extended far enough from the corner of his eye to twine up behind his ear and into his hair as if to camouflage itself there. It poked up a bit more, like a periscope.

"We love you love you worm-queen."

"Oh, that's so sweet. I love you, too, Dylan." The eerie moment had passed and she reached over briefly to stroke his mucus-smudged cheek.

"No," Dylan replied, "no – you love us. Queen loves all us all us."

"Okay, okay," she sighed, facing forward as she navigated through the center of town. "I love all of you." Encourage him – them – with whatever worked. As Paula had told the reporter, "that means not only directing our children's minds constructively, but directing the worms' minds constructively along with them."

Dylan leaned as far over as his seatbelt would allow, so as to rest his head against her arm. She was very touched by this affection, but shivered for a second as she felt a slithering damp caress along her elbow.

"Sit up now, honey, we're almost home," she told him.

Endure, she thought, smiling tightly into the night. Endure.

ADORATION

Carpet of rain-slicked leaves, black and glossy as flesh swollen with rot, trees like fossilized lightning stabbed into the earth, tiny pallid mushrooms like the protruding fingers of buried infants, damp sky the same dismal gray as the clapboards of the dilapidated house the two men could see ahead through the last of the scarred trunks.

They stole upon the structure from the rear as if afraid they might startle it into fleeing or disappearing. After all, it had the aura of a place that had long eluded discovery, that had been built out in this remote spot for the sake of concealment. An overgrown dirt road snaked away from its front, and must have connected with some road sooner or later, though for these men it had been easier to park their car and approach the house through a stretch of forest. McComis only half-fancifully wondered if that dirt road led off to even more secretive places – a whole town or even an entire looming city, similarly gray, similarly hidden away from all but those few souls who found the way.

They had seen no other houses along their hike. They had heard no birds, the only sign of animal habitation being a high, strange chittering. Startled by its suddenness, McComis had looked above and around him for its owner.

"Red squirrel," Dore had explained. "They like to scold you."

But McComis had been doubtful. The sound had contained something of the insect in it, and yet also the suggestion of a human child's voice.

At the perimeter of the property there was a trace of ancient stone wall – half buried and the rest, like vertebrae jutting from the earth, smothered in lush plants – against which little white clusters of lilies-of-the-valley stood out. Those tiny, delicate bells had been McComis' mother's favorite flower; it grew in shadowed places.

The two men stepped over the wall and into a tiny clearing filled by the house. It was utterly drained of color, slats fallen from its sides in places, holes gaping in its eaves where birds or squirrels – or whatever had made that angry sound – no doubt took refuge in the colder months, which were poised to descend seemingly at any moment.

McComis followed Dore around to the front of the two-storey house. Its windows were all blinded by shades like eyelids fallen in death, though McComis wondered what might be peering at him around their frayed edges.

They mounted a few steps, but before he knocked on the door Dore opened the front of his expensive jacket to show McComis the handle of the semi-automatic pistol tucked in his waistband, indenting his swollen belly. McComis had thought before that the man had more the look of a gangster than a businessman, and now that image was only heightened. Dore buttoned his jacket again.

"Just so you know I'm able to protect you. You won't need me to protect you, so long as you stick to the rules we've discussed, but I just want to reassure you. Don't be afraid, okay? I'm right here. Nothing's going to happen to you...if you just stick to the program."

McComis nodded, and swallowed what felt like a sea urchin. "I understand."

Dore stared at him another moment, and then turned to rap on the door.

It opened almost instantly, as if the opener had been on the other side listening to their exchange. And as the door swung inward, gray light fell on a shadowed face and McComis felt his already trotting heart surge forward as if to dash itself to death against his ribs.

The man who stood in the doorway was dead, seemingly as long dead as the house itself, and in fact both looked as if they had never been alive. His flesh was not purplish but purple, purple and slick as that of an eggplant, except where it was torn or ulcerated, in which places it had a white crustiness. The eyes were so caked in bright yellow scabs that McComis wondered if the corpse had vision, or navigated by other senses. But its haircut was fairly neat, and its suit was no less expensive that those of the two living men.

The creature stepped back to permit their entrance. It didn't stagger, didn't seem sluggish in its movements. McComis would have preferred it to be less coordinated. Without a word to the thing, Dore moved past it, into the house's interior. McComis followed swiftly, keeping his gaze straight ahead but shuddering as his sleeve brushed that of the dead man.

In the short hallway there was a staircase to the second floor. At its head was another dead man, of the same general appearance except that this one was obese, though whether he had been that way in life or if he were expanded with the gases of decomposition, McComis couldn't guess. The corpse waved an arm to indicate they should mount the steps, and Dore did so. McComis trailed behind after darting a furtive look over his shoulder.

There were no lights on in the house. No music or TV played. Still as a mausoleum, its atmosphere damp as that of a basement, the smell of mold strong from the brown, water-stained and sloughing wallpaper. Past the obese cadaver, the two visitors passed along another hallway, forgoing several closed doors in favor of the door at its end. There, a third dead man awaited them. This one, too, stepped aside to permit their entrance. But this time, Dore did not enter. He hung back, and McComis looked to him.

"Go on," Dore prompted him, even smiling. "This is what you paid for."

Yes...and he had paid a lot. But now he wasn't so sure he wanted to see what his money had bought him. He wouldn't ask for it back, or he was sure that Dore – or the others – wouldn't let him leave alive (and then would he himself become a fourth "body" guard?). He would let Dore keep the money. He just didn't think he could go through with this.

But the door was already open. Dore waited expectantly. Stick to the program, Dore had warned him. Wheels were already in motion.

McComis stepped through the threshold. The door snicked shut discreetly behind him.

There was a large bed at the center of the small room, a bed that loomed like a planet with an atmosphere of sickly sweet perfume, somewhat musty like the petals of dying roses. And in this expanse, this vastness of bed, in a shimmer of silk nightgown, reclined Marilyn Monroe.

Her flesh was not purple, festered with sores. It was creamy-smooth and softly luminous as if it were filmed through a smear of Vaseline, to soften the effects of age. But it was not a glowing ghost he saw. Her toenails were actually painted. Her full, voluptuous body physically depressed the mattress. Her eyes were not crusted in yellow pus, but shone at McComis, narrowed in a smile.

"Hi, honey," she breathed. She ran her hand across the mattress in little circles. "Come on in...don't be shy." That trademark wispy little girl voice.

McComis had had a crush on Marilyn Monroe from childhood. She might have been his first of many celebrity crushes, and though he had other favorites now, Marilyn was the ultimate celebrity, wasn't she? An icon. A goddess. Immortal.

And yet, for all her beauty, he feared her more than the dead men. They, at least, were honest about their condition. And he had never intended to touch the dead men. But he was here to touch the flesh of this woman. To press his lips to it. To enter the most vulnerable part of him into it. Might the decay, the wretchedness, be lurking deviously within? Though how could she appear so healthy, so alive on the outside, if the fruit were rotten at its core?

She patted the mattress. "Come on, baby...I won't bite." She giggled. "Unless you want me to." And as she shifted, a strap of her nightgown slipped off the smooth roundness of her shoulder.

McComis again nearly choked on a barbed, dried ball of saliva. But he took one step further into the room. He had been resting his back against the closed door for support. Now, free of it, he felt like he might totter and fall, and he seemed to stagger toward the bed against his will, drawn by the planet's gravity. Marilyn slid over to make room for him, still smiling. The idol of millions for decades, but it was him she wanted. Him...

Still staggering those few steps to the great bed, he saw her slip her nightgown up over her head. Nipples pink as if flushed with living blood. Nipples pink against lush white flesh like rose petals fallen on the marble of a gravestone.

But she was not cold, like stone, when he touched her at last. Warm...soft...so warm and soft...

* * *

"Well?" Dore asked, still smiling. Had he been smiling all the while, these past few hours? Lingering outside the door with the dead man, both of them listening?

McComis didn't tell him how it had been. "Let's go," he murmured. But as he started ahead of Dore down the hall, his back to the other man, he said, "I'll be back next week."

"Marilyn again?"

"No," McComis said – quietly, as if she might hear him and be hurt, though he wasn't sure she was even in that room anymore. In the house anymore. Had she already been returned to wherever it was she had been summoned or conjured from?

"Lady Di? Selena?" Dore brought forth their names with a hint of enthusiasm that suggested he had enjoyed the products of this place himself.

The idea of calling up such recently deceased celebrities nauseated McComis for some reason. It made them too real, whereas Marilyn was almost the stuff of myth; harder to imagine she had ever been a real living person, a child, a corpse.

"No," he said. "Maybe Grace Kelly. Maybe Carole Lombard." More goddesses. More myths.

"Those old movie broads were too chubby for my tastes," opined the paunchy Dore. He lit a cigarette as they descended the stairs.

Outside it had begun to drizzle again, but McComis welcomed the open air. Despite the moldering of the leaves beneath their feet. At least it cleared his head of the delirious scent of rose petals. He only wished Dore would quicken his pace through the forest, before they became lost out here when night fell, which must have been imminent.

"How did you find this place?" McComis asked him while they walked.

"I can't tell you stuff like that. Look...I didn't find it; it was shown to me. I have a boss I answer to, like I told you before. Someone like you. Someone with money. Somebody who could have anything he wanted. In other words, somebody really bored. I think he might have made the place, somehow. Or I mean, made it into the place that it is. With enough money, you can make anything happen, if you hook up with the right people with the right knowledge. I don't know much more than you, and I can't tell you any more about the man I work for."

"Does anyone besides me and him come here?"

"There are a few other clients."

"Who do they ask for?"

"Marilyn has been called before," he said, grinning over at McComis as if he thought he might be jealous. "But not just movie stars. One guy wanted Joan of Arc, and Cleopatra, but they wouldn't come. Either they're too long gone, or it has to be someone whose image is really clear in your mind, like a rock star or a TV celebrity. One guy calls up male actors. James Dean. Elvis Presley. Elvis looked great – I saw him. And they never refuse. They always act like they want it. Elvis would've kicked the shit out of this guy if he tried that stuff when he was alive, but dead folk don't say no."

"In life they had all that adoration," McComis mused aloud.

"Yeah, that could be it. They miss that. Maybe they need it, to stay alive in our minds. I don't know. I don't know if it's even really them, or a kind of recording. A videotape. But they're flesh – you know that."

McComis didn't respond. But yes, he knew that. He had ultimately kissed Marilyn passionately, his tongue in her mouth, her mouth moist with saliva inside. So moist inside...

✦   ✦   ✦

He rented a video with Marilyn Monroe, but after fifteen minutes he had to turn it off.

Alone in his house, watching the movie, it had frightened him too much, as if it had been those three animated dead men he'd seen captured on celluloid.

Alone in his house – yes. He had been divorced for three years now. His wife had since remarried. A pretty woman; he doubted she would have married a plain-looking man like himself in the first place, had it not been for his money. He had never been good with dating. He experienced romance vicariously, through film. But then, didn't most people? Did anyone's life approach the glamour of fabrication?

It was his mother, he felt, who had inspired his love of movies, particularly older movies. Bette Davis had been her favorite actress. Watching these women always brought his mother to the front of his mind, as if she were the actual star of each film; their immortality lent her a wispy immortality, too. She had been a pretty woman herself; photos of the poet Anne Sexton put him in mind of his mother. The lean tapered face, the dark hair, the pale intelligent eyes.

His mother had passed away from breast cancer when McComis was twelve years old.

Thinking of her now, he wanted to go dig out his scrapbooks, filled with photos of her. But instead, he stared at the blank television screen with a slowly mounting intensity, as if he expected to suddenly hear the tape machine begin to whir again, and it would be his mother's face he would see on the screen, once again alive.

* * *

"She's waiting for you," said Dore. Smiling.

McComis locked his eyes with the man for several beats. Dore began digging for a cigarette, breaking their gaze. McComis then turned and let himself into the bedroom.

A woman stood silhouetted at the window, peeking out secretly around the torn shade. At his entrance, she turned. Her slender frame was draped in a light, flowered summer dress. Dark hair, limned in the light from the window in a nearly extinguished corona.

"Oh, honey," the woman cooed, stepping away from the window. "Oh, Tom...baby...how I've missed you." She held her arms open to him. "How I've missed you, all these years."

And he found himself staggering to her, again drawn as if against his conscious will, but some part of him obviously anxious, desperate, in need. McComis fell into the youthful arms of his mother, dead for these many years but not aged a day since he'd last seen her. And he crushed her in his arms, as hers went around him. It was the smell of her familiar lily-of-the-valley perfume, ultimately, that made him cry.

"I've missed you, too," he sobbed in her hair, against her slim throat. "I've missed you, too." He bucked hard with his sobs, and she kissed his neck to soothe him, ran her hands across his back.

"Shh, it's all right now, darling," she whispered. "We're together now."

"I think about you all the time, but I never dreamed I could see you again...I never dreamed..."

"I know," she sighed. "We need each other, don't we? I've dreamed of you, too. I can still remember holding you as a baby in my arms. Breast-feeding you. And now, at last, here we are again. You in my arms." She gently pushed him out of their embrace, her hands running tenderly down his chest. She unfastened the one button that held his jacket closed, and began to slip it off his shoulders. "We don't have to be alone anymore."

McComis took hold of her thin wrists, held them away from him. "What are you doing?" he rasped.

His mother, now shorter than he was – yes, even a few years younger than he was – smiled up at him. "Don't worry, honey," she giggled softly. "I won't bite you. Not unless you want me to."

McComis shoved the woman away from him. She almost fell, grabbed the footboard of the bed for support. He in turn backed away from her, against the door.

"You aren't my mother!" he cried.

"Of course I am, Tom!" She still smiled, despite his violence, her pale eyes hungry. Hungry for his love.

"My mother wouldn't do that! And I never loved my mother like that!"

"Every woman a man loves is really his mother, Tom."

McComis whirled around to grapple with the doorknob.

"What are you doing?" his mother demanded, floating suddenly toward him. "Wait!"

He finally got the knob turned – he mustn't let her touch him – and was out through the door, slamming it in her face. Her heard her slight but solid body thud against it, heard her pound the heels of her fists against it.

"Tom!" she wailed. "Come back! Please – I need you!"

"What's wrong?" Dore asked, alarmed, straightening up warily. The dead man, as well, swivelled about to face him.

But McComis plunged between them, bolted down the hall.

"Isn't that want you wanted?" Dore asked, trailing after him.

*   *   *

This time, McComis made his way to the house in the woods without his escort. He knew the secret, unmarked path through the forest by now. Dore wasn't even aware of this excursion.

In each hand, McComis lugged a heavy red container filled with gasoline. In one pocket was a tin of lighter fluid, in the other a disposable lighter. And in his own waistband, a semi-automatic handgun.

He saw it through the trees, gray beneath a gray sky. Just before he entered the clearing he heard that chittering scolding sound again. An alarm, a warning? He expected to see one of the sentries come around the edge of the house then, but none did. Still, he mustn't take any chances. He worked swiftly, uncapping the first container and splashing the outside of the house, working his way entirely around it.

Did she watch him through the bedroom window, peeking around the shade? Golden Marilyn? Tragic Jean Harlow? His mother? And were they, perhaps, really all the same creature, or merely made the same by their desperate longing?

Finally, he emptied the lighter fluid in a short trail, like a fuse. And crouching down, he lit it. The flames began to spread, an invasion of bright light and bright color in this bleak, ashen spot.

He backed off quickly and pulled the pistol from his waistband, lest something come blundering out from the interior, howling and grasping for his throat.

And as the flames spread and engulfed the old structure, began to consume it in their own greedy lust, he did in fact see one of the dead men smash its upper body through one of the windows, extend its arms toward him threateningly, its mouth wide and full of fire – but it made no sound, and after only several seconds it fell back inside the house with the inferno closing over it. He lowered the gun he had been pointing at the thing.

He returned his attention to the upper floor. The bedroom window. He saw no face at the glass, no imploring arms reached for him. He did, however, believe he heard one pitiful cry – just briefly. Yet it sounded too far away, much farther away than the house directly before him.

Tears began to fill his eyes and they reflected the wavering light of the flames, until he became blinded by the two. But he wiped his sleeve across them. He had to hurry now, back to his car, drive away and make a call, report the fire before it spread into the forest. Get away before Dore should come and find him. Not that he really cared about either of those things too greatly. Most of all, he just wanted to leave here. He wished he had never come here in the first place. But he couldn't change that, could he?

Despite the conflagration, he knew the past could be resurrected much more readily than it could be destroyed.

STAR EST CONTROL

M. Prague wasn't required to paint his toenails the same color as his fingernails, but he believed that his attention to such details was what had earned him his rank at the Registry of Faces in the first place. His fingernail color – dark brown – was a visual indication of that rank.

With his recently acquired promotion and increased salary had come his decision to move out of his one room in a boarding house for men, and take this two room apartment instead. At least his new apartment had its own toilet. That was the second room. The first was a combination livingroom/kitchenette, the two sections being partly partitioned by a counter top. His sofa folded out into a bed. It was on the edge of the bed that he sat with cotton balls between his toes, the smell of the nail polish seeming to shellac the interiors of his nostrils. It was giving him a deep and intensely focused pain just behind his right eyebrow.

To exacerbate this headache, there was a lime green light flashing at him from the corner of his eye in a kind of fluorescent semaphore. He looked up at it directly, in annoyance, to see what was silently clamoring for his attention.

Prague's flat was made more affordable because it featured advertising screens on much of its available wall space. One entire wall was a single great billboard, but most of the other screens were smaller, generally rectangular in shape but with a few squares and ovals. These banners were ranked one above the other, and end to end, from floor to ceiling. There were none on the ceiling or floor, though his landlord had shown him one of those flats (even more affordable, but Prague had felt vertiginous and vaguely guilty walking across the huge smiling face of a pretty girl advertising colored eye dyes).

His landlord had advised him not to block too many of the banners with an overabundance of furniture, but Prague only had his couch/bed, one worn armchair, and a small kitchen table with one chair, in any case. He had positioned the armchair, kitchen set and even the sofa away from the walls. He had been instructed that he could hang no pictures of his own over the advertisements, and was prohibited from hiding them with hangings or screens. His landlord had reassured him that when he went to sleep at night, a sensor would take note and the banners would be extinguished.

Some of the banners remained fixed in content, while others were animated or alternated their subject matter on rotation. The large billboard ran a continuous loop of a pretty naked couple running across black volcanic beach sand and falling down together laughing noiselessly, close to the camera. Then some type appeared, promoting Rantac, a popular mood control medication.

But the lime green that spiked Prague's skull and turned his eye was an oblong banner close to the ceiling, near to the kitchen section. That color was atrocious – too bright, too unnatural. An invented color, not one evolved in nature. Lime was just the best he could think of to describe it.

Against this green flashing field were simply the words, in bold black caps: IT'S OK TO EAT!

A public service announcement, he decided...probably against excessive dieting, or fast-paced workers not taking the time. Or maybe it was an error, an incomplete message, a broken loop for some restaurant. He had seen glitches in the banners before. One banner for dog food that had previously shown a dog running got stuck so that the dog seemed to be twitching in one spot in an electrified spasm, his tongue hanging out. And one morning just as Prague awoke, and the sensor turned on the light and color in a riot around him, an overly-amplified voice had boomed out from one of the screens. The voice had shouted, "Velvetdew – because you both deserve it!"

He had been shown, but declined, an even more affordable apartment where the advertisements took turns speaking and playing music. But he had not complained about this isolated episode to his landlord, as it had not been repeated, and M. Prague wasn't one to readily voice complaint, anyway – another reason why, he felt, he had been given his promotion at the Registry of Faces.

* * *

The light of the morning sun, however diffused by the gray winding sheet of the sky, made M. Prague squint when he emerged from his tenement building to walk to his bus stop. He tucked his chin to his chest against the morning chill and started on his way. He wanted to be early. He had never been late. He was terrified of being late. What if the bus came too soon and he missed it, or not soon enough, and he arrived tardy at the Registry of Faces? He quickened his pace.

The city reared around him in a forest of black stalagmites. Chimneys stout or slim jutted, loomed or tottered in profusion. Indeed, the leaning tapered buildings themselves seemed like the immense crumbling chimneys of vaster structures unseen beneath street level. The gray sky rippled with invisible vapors from the many lofty openings, as if a multitude of souls escaped from a ranked army of the dying.

A white form snaked between Prague's legs as he darted along the warped sidewalk. He almost stumbled. The sensuous coiling of a cat, he thought. A white cat. He shot a look over his shoulder, saw it hadn't been a cat. The ghost of a cat, maybe: the luminous white form was lifting into the air, wriggling eel-like, a tatter of ectoplasm. Prague faced front again and walked even faster.

As he approached a street intersection, nearly at his stop now, more of those white swimming forms emerged from around the corner, directly in front of him. His pace faltered, but before he could duck into a doorway or cross the street to avoid them, the glowing fish-like shapes swarmed around him. They were more like fish skeletons than fish – bare, plucked things. He realized, then, that they were words. Holographic ads, sent out like carrier pigeons. Were they meant to flock together like this or should they have dispersed? He blinked, batted at them, though of course he made no contact. An attractive woman with a blood-red kerchief framing her face smirked at him in a way he didn't like, but he averted his eyes from her and continued on his way.

Only a few of the ghostly ads, rippling like flags, persisted in following him, harassing him, now that they had his scent. He did his best not to give them the satisfaction of a look, but at last he glanced at the nearest of them and took in its message:

STAR EST CONTROL

It took him several moments to digest this. He might not have interpreted its meaning, had he not been familiar with an extermination service named Star Pest Control, not far from his office. A closer inspection of the other floating banners behind and around him confirmed that all of them were similarly defective, maimed, missing the "P" in "Pest". Was nothing ever whole, untainted?

Prague had rounded the corner now, and lost all but one tenacious banner, luckily falling behind him. He saw his bus stop ahead. The bus wasn't there – was that good or bad? Nestled up to the curb almost in the bus's space was a truck that carried a trash dumpster on its back – either picking up a full one or dropping off an empty one. Prague was distressed; was there room enough for the bus to pull in? He should see if a constable were about, and complain.

The dumpster was painted a vivid red, and it had an opening at its end, which faced Prague. A tarp was pinned over the opening, hanging down a bit in the middle so that over the top of it he could see the black of the metal box's interior. The sagging tarp was colored the exact same red as the metal body of the dumpster – thus, Prague had at first mistaken the rumpled tarp for a badly damaged metal door, crumpled in some terrible impact. The illusion didn't trouble him much, but the color was a bit offensive to him – too loud, too strong.

But even as he approached the truck, it gave a hiss and a rumble and pulled away from the curb, entering into traffic. Taking his spot of sidewalk, the precise spot he claimed every morning, he watched the red dumpster wind its way amongst the smaller, darker, beetle-like vehicles of other workers on their morning migration. Why must a dumpster announce itself so garishly? That red was appalling.

He waited ten minutes for the bus. It came on time. Prague's bunched shoulders lowered ever so slightly. While waiting, he had alternated between glancing at his pocket watch and stealing peeks at a young couple waiting for the bus beside him. Well, perhaps they weren't a romantic couple, maybe just co-workers. Both wore charcoal-colored baggy suits. Hers looked a bit frayed, like her hair. Bottom rung clerks, he inwardly sneered. And he flicked his eyes to the fore again when the man touched the woman's arm in the midst of their conversation. Very unbecoming, such obvious flirtation.

When the bus pulled up with a great belch of wavering invisible vapor, Prague checked to see if the solitary banner still hounded him. No sign of it. Relieved, he boarded the bus, mounting its steps directly behind the woman in the worn suit. He took a deep inhalation, and caught the scent of her jagged hair.

✶　✶　✶

The black beach sand clung to their pale, youthful flesh with its sheen of healthy sweat, like obsidian pulverized to powder, as if the young naked couple lay embracing in the ash of a vaporized city. This city. They laughed noiselessly as the huge banner screen superimposed text over them which advertised RANTAC – TO KEEP YOU IN BALANCE.

Though he lay in his fold-out sofa-bed, beneath the covers, the banners had not yet extinguished themselves because Prague was not asleep. His hand worked rhythmically under his blanket, so that it looked like the rolling waves at the edge of that obsidian beach. His eyes were more fixed on the girl tonight. Sometimes he focused more on the equally perfect young man.

Before the laughing, embracing couple could actually begin to make love, they were gone...only to appear once again on the horizon, running toward the camera – toward Prague – hand in hand. Her breasts bounced. The man's member flopped. Prague's eyes and mouth were open like a dead man's. Only his hand moved.

But soon enough he turned away in disgust, closed his eyes against the screen and the profusion of smaller banners, curling himself in a fetal position and drawing the edge of the blanket over his head. Until he actually fell asleep, the banners would glow, and their glow kept him from sleep. He wished he had a button to shut them all off. He felt their colored gaze on him. He heard the soundless laughter of that too-perfect, too-happy couple.

✳   ✳   ✳

His new desk at the Registry of Faces was inclined slightly like a drafting table, with a strip of buttons and dials along either side of a large monitor screen set in a circular frame of glossy cherry wood. His desk was in a cubicle like a tiny apartment flat without a ceiling. Its walls were empty but for a few memos; he frowned upon the unprofessional decor in his neighbors' cubicles. One woman had a calendar of naked men with dogs' heads superimposed onto their necks. This woman had an irritating laugh, and talked too much, and Prague wondered how she had ever achieved her status. She didn't even paint her nails with the color of her office rank, used a lurid blood red instead.

He tuned out her chatter, and the loud coughing of a man in one of the cubicles that were suspended from the ceiling and accessed by a complex catwalk system. (There were three levels of these suspended cubicles; Prague was afraid that one day, the cubicle nearest to the high ceiling would tear free, and crash into the one directly below it, and so on, sending a whole train of cubicles down upon his head.) He blocked out all else, kept his eyes focused on the circular monitor, watching a succession of photographed faces. Each visage lingered before him for ten seconds unless he altered the rate or paused it entirely.

Because he was presently viewing a succession of Oriental women, the Caucasian woman took him by surprise. Not that he thought all Oriental women looked the same. One's face would be narrow, the next one's broad, long hair, short hair, but there was a sameness in that they were all female, all dark-haired, all almond-eyed, so that sometimes it seemed it was one single Oriental woman whose head was pulsing and undulating, ceaselessly molding itself.

But what also surprised him about this Caucasian intruder was that hers was obviously the face of a dead woman.

He touched a button to pause the image.

The source of her injuries – assuming she hadn't died of disease – was not apparent, but there was no mistaking the milky emptiness of the staring eyes, the slack but frozen gape of her mouth. The photograph was a poor one, the color dull, the focus a touch off, unlike the clarity of the ones he had been viewing. All those almond eyes gazing directly at him. These eyes looked off to the side, to an oblivion just over his shoulder.

It was misfiled, that was all. A clerical mistake.

Prague glanced furtively over his shoulder, as if to see what the young, pretty dead woman was staring at. He then faced forward again, darted his hand out and flicked a metal toggle. The photograph of the dead woman was deleted from the file, and replaced with the next solemn Oriental face.

✳   ✳   ✳

He was dreaming. The banners were dark, but he was still being watched...

In the dream, he was naked, and much thinner than he should be – nearly skeletal. He was trudging across a desert of endless flatness, a desert of fine black glittering powder, with no ocean in sight. He was pulling something heavy behind him. The hissing of this burden across the sand was deafening.

He was pulling an entire city behind him, as if it were built upon a vast sled. And this black, jagged city was connected to his head, as if it were an immense tumor that had emanated from his very body. It was tethered to the back of his head by a thick cord of flesh, pulled taut but not tearing. He leaned his whole body forward with the effort, dragging the city onward...onward...

He couldn't turn his head to see the city behind him. Or perhaps he was simply forbidden to do so. Or afraid. But somehow he knew that there was a figure standing in every doorway, a face pressed to each and every window in every tottering tower. He sensed infinite sets of eyes, all staring directly at him. And he pulled all these eyes along behind him...across the barren landscape...

✴   ✴   ✴

When the bus pulled up to the curb this morning, the banner that ran the length of it said YOU'LL BE SORRY.

Sorry, if what? Prague wondered. He had missed the start of the message...either that, or a glitch prevented the rest of it from playing. The banner went dark after that. If the message resumed, he was already on the bus by then.

Sorry if he didn't buy this product? Subscribe to that service? Take this pharmaceutical?

As the bus jolted into movement once more, and Prague was rocked in his seat, he noticed that he hadn't seen that couple again, who were either romantically involved or co-workers or both – the young man, and the girl with the frayed suit and hair.

A peripheral movement caught his eye. It looked like snow, or a drift of dandelion seeds. He looked out his smeared, blurred window and saw the insect-like swarm of free-floating ads for Star Pest Control again. They were outdistanced so quickly that he couldn't tell if the "P" had been restored in them. He found himself sinking down in his seat a bit, as if afraid they would see him in the bus, and give chase.

✴   ✴   ✴

Today it was a succession of children's faces. Some looked ready to laugh, others to cry. Most looked serious and resigned. Then, suddenly in their midst, the face of a man with his eyes gouged out.

His face had been washed afterwards, so there was no blood. Perhaps that made it worse. Yawning eyes contrasting horribly with the calm, close-lipped mouth. He was young, had apparently been good-looking.

How could anyone be so careless as to allow these files to become improperly inserted this way? Perhaps it was the red-nailed ninny in the neighboring booth.

His heart still trotted from the shock. Prague flicked a look over his shoulder, then up at the vertical stack of cubicles above him, then hunched over the monitor as if to blot it with his body and flipped the toggle to erase the image...but even as it vanished, replaced by the glum features of a little red-haired boy, he regretted not studying the photo a moment or two longer. Maybe it was only because he had been thinking about the man that very morning, but in that last second he had imagined the murdered man and the young man he had seen at the bus stop were one and the same.

And if so, did that make the woman...

He wouldn't allow himself to complete the thought. It was not them. Why would it be?

But for the rest of the afternoon, Prague had to slow the rate of faces down from ten seconds to thirty seconds each, thus getting behind in his work – which he had never done before – because he found it hard to focus on the countenances passing before him. He kept seeing two other faces, superimposed by his memory.

*   *   *

He stood at the counter that partially divided the one large room of his flat into the illusion of two. He was slicing the end off a loaf of bread, but found its crust hard and flaking, the interior crunchy. Stale. He set down the knife beside the bread, and for a moment lost himself in the way a luminous banner was reflected in the bright metal. Backwards words advertised a new lipstick. Gray and blue were the hues in fashion. A woman's blue lips parted on the surface of the blade.

Abruptly, as if he had peripherally sensed a change, he thrust his gaze up at the one large billboard that advertised Rantac. A new advertisement showed there instead. He was so accustomed to the old ad that the new image before him blanked his mind and transfixed his eyes, like an animal caught in headlights.

On the huge banner there was a red wall, and in the center of this red – metal – wall was an opening. A dark doorway. It appeared as if a metal panel had been dented and twisted and wrenched away from that doorway, but in fact it was simply that a red-colored tarp had been hung across the opening, and it sagged down in the middle, showing just the top of the black recess behind it.

There was no text. No movement. Just this. But no...was there a dim white glow, after all, moving in the blackness behind the drooping tarpaulin? Yes...yes, there was. A vague pale figure. And it drew nearer to the opening. It peered out at him from over the top of the curtain, yet he couldn't make out the shadowed face, the dark – too dark – eyes. But a hand emerged, and curled its fingers around the top edge of the tarp. The fingernails of this hand were lacquered a dark brown.

Prague clapped his palms over his eyes, as if to press those gelatinous orbs all the way into his skull. As if to flatten them against the wall of his brain. But it was the soundlessness that made him look again. If there had been an accompanying sound or noise, even just a rustle of plastic tarp, he would know if it were all over or still looming before him. But the silence...that could go on forever.

When he lowered his palms several inches, he saw the young couple high on love and Rantac racing toward him naked, hands linked, arms and legs lithe and long, smooth and lubricated in perspiration.

Prague lowered his arms the rest of the way, and then noticed a smaller banner off to his right, lodged between a diminutive window and the much-locked door to his flat. The rectangular, horizontal display showed a woman's leg. An ad for pantyhose? Hair removal? He found himself scuffing in his slippers closer to the banner to see it more clearly, his hands now tucked in the pockets of the white robe he wore over his neat white pajamas against his apartment's constant chill.

Yes, it was a woman's leg. Sleek and snowy and perfect as alabaster. The leg of a statue. A leg broken off a statue. Because the leg ended at the upper thigh, in a ragged wound that had been washed so that the blood would not mar the perfection of that smooth, silken white skin. The neatly trimmed nails of the delicate, child-like toes had been meticulously painted a deep shade of brown.

Prague turned his head. Most of the banners were normal. Bland. Almost reassuring where once they had harassed him, tugged and prodded at him. Across the room, however, he thought he saw a man's hand and forearm on a small banner between two kitchen cupboards. This time he didn't want to approach it. But a screen very close to his face when he whirled around showed a glistening formless mass on a shiny kitchen counter top. This image had text where the others hadn't. Red letters scrolled down from the top of the banner and read: THIS IS NOT YOUR KIDNEY.

Stumbling away from the wall, out into the center of the room, Prague whipped his head this way and then that, but when he looked again at each of the terrible banners, they had changed to advertise a shoe store, a jewelry store, a new dieting book.

Was that a tiny scratch or tap at the window behind him? How could it be, up here, above ground level? There were no tree branches near to the building.

Prague confronted the glass, and through his ghost-white reflection he saw a glowing, writhing eel-like shape hovering at the pane. The rippling words read STAR EST CONTROL.

He rushed to the window and drew down its ragged shade like an eyelid.

* * *

On his fold-out sofa-bed, M. Prague lay curled in a fetus-like position...naked and pale as a worm, his damp flesh pimpled and doughy – but his finger and toenails were meticulously, freshly painted.

The smell of the polish made his head scream with pain.

He peeked over his arm, and saw the one large screen for Rantac. The inviting beach now looked forbidding. The sun was setting, nearly extinguished. A breeze that he imagined to be cool, chilly, blew the black sand about like the ash of a crematorium.

The young couple were gone.

Prague would not peek at the many smaller banners all around him, but from each and every one of them he sensed a face staring at him. Some staring accusingly without eyes.

He closed his own eyes, wet with tears.

If he could only fall asleep...

If he could just fall asleep, the sensor would know, and those faces might go away.

ABOUT THE AUTHORS

JEFF STRAND is the creator of Andrew Mayhem, whose demented adventures appear in the novels *Graverobbers Wanted (No Experience Necessary)*, *Single White Psychopath Seeks Same, Casket For Sale (Only Used Once)*, and also in the hit-man anthology *These Guns For Hire.*

His other novels include the giant-killer-ants-on-a-rampage extravaganza *Mandibles*, the feel-good zombie novel *The Sinister Mr. Corpse*, and his first "serious" novel *Pressure*, which *Publishers Weekly* and other fine critics said did not suck at all. He's also responsible for a trio of comedy novels where nobody gets dismembered: *Out of Whack*, *Elrod McBugle on the Loose*, and *How to Rescue a Dead Princess.*

His short story collection *Gleefully Macabre Tales* is coming soon. Or, depending when you're reading this, is already out. Or, depending on his career trajectory, has just been canceled by the publisher in a momentary fit of rational thought.

You can visit his Seriously Whacked website at www.jeffstrand.com, and you'd be plumb foolish not to.

ADAM PEPPER'S debut novel, *Memoria* received rave reviews from *Cemetery Dance*, *Chronicle* and *Chizine*. He's drawn praise from genre veterans F. Paul Wilson, Thomas Monteleone and Tom Piccirilli for his unique brand of dark fiction. His short stories have appeared in *Scars*, *Decadence* and *Best of Horrorfind, Vol. 2*. Adam heads up the New York City chapter of the Horror Writers Association.

Learn more about Adam at www.adampepper.com.

SARAH PINBOROUGH lives in Milton Keynes, England and is the author of four novels, *The Hidden, The Reckoning, Breeding Ground* and *The Taken.*
  She is currently working on a TV screenplay, two novels and a novella and has short stories coming out during 2007 in anthologies from Carrol and Graf and Cemetery Dance.
  You can find out more about Sarah's work at her website www.sarahpinborough.com or at www.myspace.com/sarahpinborough.

JEFFREY THOMAS is the author of the novels *Deadstock, A Nightmare on Elm Street: The Dream Dealers, Letters From Hades, Boneland, The Sea of Flesh and Ash* (with Scott Thomas), *Everybody Scream!* and *Monstrocity,* which was nominated for a Bram Stoker Award. His collections include *Punktown, Doomsdays, Unholy Dimensions, AAAIIIEEE!!!* and *Thirteen Specimens.* He has appeared in the anthologies *The Year's Best Horror Stories XXII, The Year's Best Fantasy and Horror #14, A Walk on the Darkside, Lost on the Darkside* and *The Solaris Book of New Science Fiction.*
  His official web site is www.jeffreyethomas.com.